Isaac MAMPUYA Samba,

Presents:

© 2019: Diagram drawn by Isaac MAMPUYA Samba.

IRENE AND AN OTHER FORM OF TORTURE OF HER OWN CONSCIENCE (CONTINUATION)

Isaac **MAMPUYA** Samba

TRANSLATED FROM THE FRENCH TO AMERICAN
BY HIMSELF THE AUTHOR ISAAC MAMPUYA SAMBA
Doctor of Es' Letters (Paris-Sorbonne)

ISBN: 978-1-63950-330-8 (sc)
ISBN: 978-1-63950-332-2 (e)

Writers Apex

Gateway Towards Success

8063 MADISON AVE #1252
Indianapolis, IN 46227
+13176596889
www.writersapex.com

THE CONTINUATION OF THE HIKING'S LITERARY "IsMaSa" TO PERPETUATE ITSELF IN:

"IRENE AND AN OTHER FORM OF TORTURE OF HER OWN CONSCIENCE" (CONTINUATION)

REVIEW AND CORRECTED. BRIEF: "A NEW GREAT HIGH – QUALITY" OF: "IRENE AND AN OTHER FORM OF TORTURE OF HER OWN CONSCIENCE". (CONTINUATION).

As Info (Communication): In fact, "IRENE" as such: there are 4 in all; and this one turns out to be IRENE N°4. Please – therefore, Readers, also wait for the REPUBLICATIONS of THREE other EPISODES of IRENE, REVISED AND CORRECTED; which will be released with the Company of Madame Tina Mills, of: Writers Apex Gateway Success Address: 1309 Coffeen Avenue STE 1200 Sheridan, WY 82801 USA.

The Fate had thus arranged for the paths of a certain Irene LUCINDAÇIO and a certain Almeida LOURENÇO to cross. But here's the thing: between the Two of them, there's going to be some dagger-drawn excitement.

————COINCIDENCE?

————Maybe so!

————Or even maybe not!

But nevertheless, after .../...

THE AUTHOR

Isaac MAMPUYA Samba, the Boy of the Commune of Ndjili (in Kinshasa: Democratic Republic of Congo).

THE KEY WORDS OF VOLUME

ALBERTO is someone who passes in a span of time:

from the good atmosphere of "hymeneal" understanding, to a formidable aggressiveness;

then: from the dreaded aggressiveness, to euphoria;

then: from the euphoria, to the lethargy;

and then the course is easily reversed with him ALBERTO; since, we often notice, he goes from the lethargy, to the euphoria;

from the euphoria, to the dreaded aggressiveness;

from the formidable aggressiveness, to the good climate of matrimonial harmony.

That's a problem with him ALBERTO!

It's a really big deal with him!

Yes, in a relationship, ALBERTO, it is ultimately a real problem; a real, real problem!

I, IRENE, by the way, I am the solution so to speak; a real solution!

But only here, I prefer to be me; rather than him; I prefer to be the solution; rather: than be the real problem!

But only there it is, him ALBERTO with his pig character; him ALBERTO with his real problem; from now on, he only has to look for the solution elsewhere; and no more question, at home, definitely!

Irene Lucindaçio and Alberto Rodriguez, as a result of the outrages, which ones, they themselves had committed; they would be Para - Normally speaking, Mysteriously, persecuted and tormented.

If Mademoiselle Irene LUCINDAÇIO had forgiven Alberto RODRIGUEZ; when there was still time; it might not have happened where we had arrived.

Where had we arrived?

At disasters, many disasters.

Where had we arrived?

To tragedies; many tragedies.

And all these catastrophes; and all these tragedies; that is to say:

The death of .../...

"From: The King of Kiosks – Literary – Romantic's – Monographic – Retrospectives And Unexplored: Isaac MAMPUYA Samba."

"**I**rene Lucindaçio had completely lost the North; completely lost the North! That's all: Completely lost the North Meticulously. Imitating supposedly, according to her, of course; of course! That's all: Of course!, Ma'am Lorena FLORINDA. Which one was doing so, the same."

"Irene Lucindaçio would stop so to speak, ever now: to reveal; to reveal; to reveal; to reveal herself indecently; to reveal; to reveal; to reveal; to reveal herself indecently! That's all: To reveal; to reveal; to reveal; to reveal herself indecently!, in the air; imitating supposedly, according to her, of course; affirmative! That's all affirmative!, Bultez SULIVAN. Which one was doing so, the same."

"to move; to move; to move; of improperly moving her body rhythmically in the air; improperly moving her body rhythmically in the air! That's all: Improperly moving her body rhythmically in the air!; imitating supposedly, according to her, of course; obviously! That's all: Obviously!, Alfonso FUKIAKANDA. Which one was doing so, the same."

"to gesticulate; to gesticulate; to gesticulate; to desperately gesticulating in the air; to desperately gesticulating in the air! That's all: To desperately gesticulating in the air!; virtually anywhere where she found herself. Imitating supposedly, according to her, of course; exactly! That's all exactly!, Adelaide Matumona. Which one was doing so, the same."

"In short really, Irene Lucindaçio used the art of the writing; used the art of the writing! That's all: Used the art of the writing. Imitating supposedly, according to her, of course; verily! That's all verily!, the writer Isaac MAMPUYA Samba. Which one was doing so, the same."

"In short really, Irene Lucindaçio bitterly spoke; bitterly spoke! That's all: Bitterly spoke!; imitating supposedly, according to her, of course; absolutely! That's all absolutely!, Imbourt GUERIN. Which one was doing so, the same."

"Irene Lucindaçio spoke irreverently; spoke irreverently! That's all: Spoke irreverently!; imitating supposedly, according to her, of course; very well! That's all: Very well!, the Pastor Fernando Bezina. Which one was doing so, the same."

"Irene Lucindaçio spoke invalidly; spoke invalidly! That's all: Spoke invalidly. Imitating supposedly, according to her, of course; that's all indeed!, agreed!, Arnold Gutenberg Which one was doing so, the same."

"In short ultimately Irene Lucindaçio spoke disdainfully; spoke disdainfully! That's all: Spoke disdainfully!; imitating supposedly, according to her, of course; that's all agreed!, indeed!, Eugenio VENSIO. Which one was doing so, the same."

"Irene Lucindaçio spoke wistfully; spoke wistfully! That's all: Spoke wistfully!; imitating supposedly, according to her, of course; surely! That's all surely!, Agostinho Miguel. Which one was doing so, the same."

"Irene Lucindaçio was speaking poorly; was speaking poorly! That's all: Was speaking poorly. Imitating supposedly, according to her, of course; that's: Oll Korrect!, Ma'am Mikaella RENNECHEO. Which one was doing so, the same."

In short now, Irene Lucindaçio sang irreparably; sang irreparably! That's all: Sang irreparably!; imitating supposedly, according to her, of course; that's all correct!, Mr. Althino FERNANDE. Which one was doing so, the same."

Irene Lucindaçio sang rudely; sang rudely! That's all: Sang rudely!; imitating supposedly, according to her, of course; of course! That's all: Of course!, Ma'am Ana Valente. Which one was doing so, the same."

"Irene Lucindaçio Huming awkwardly; Huming awkwardly! That's all: Huming awkwardly. Imitating supposedly, according to her, of course; that's all OK!, Inacio DONZILA. Which one was doing so, the same."

"In short now, Irene Lucindaçio sang irrevocably; sang irrevocably! That's all: Sang irrevocably!; imitating supposedly, according to her, of course; absolutely! That's all absolutely!, Justino Djebali. Which one was doing so, the same."

"Irene Lucindaçio sang disproportionately; sang disproportionately! That's all: Sang disproportionately!; imitating supposedly, according to her, of course; certainly! That's all: Certainly!, Haman GENSEN. Which one was doing so, the same."

"Irene Lucindaçio sang darkly; sang darkly! That's all: Sang darkly. Imitating supposedly, according to her, of course; that's all right yes!, Antonio Ferreira. Which one was doing so, the same."

"In short really, Irene Lucindaçio proved worryingly; worryingly! That's all: Worryingly!, and immodestly; immodestly! That's all: Immodestly!; imitating supposedly, according to her, of course; that's right yes!, Sebastião VARGAS. Which one was doing so, the same."

"Irene Lucindaçio proved recklessly; recklessly! That's all: Recklessly!, and shamelessly; shamelessly! That's all: Shamelessly!; imitating supposedly, according to her, of course; that's right!, Luis Soarès Gracia. Which one was doing so, the same."

"Irene Lucindaçio proved mechanically; mechanically! That's all: Mechanically!, and impulsively; impulsively! That's all: Impulsively. Imitating supposedly, according to her, of course; Oll Korrect!, Stella-Maria HOBBONE. Which one was doing so, the same."

"In short now, Irene Lucindaçio gesticulated irreparably; gesticulated irreparably! That's all: Gesticulated irreparably!; imitating supposedly, according to her, of course; that's all indeed!, Joachim MENE. Imitating supposedly, according to her, of course; that's all affirmative!, JOÃO BARRAY-Santos. Which one was doing so, the same."

"Irene Lucindaçio gesticulated pathologically; gesticulated pathologically! That's all: Gesticulated pathologically!; imitating supposedly, according to her, of course; that's all absolutely!, Manuella LUCINDAÇIO. Which one was doing so, the same."

"Irene Lucindaçio gesticulated weakly; gesticulated weakly! That's all: Gesticulated weakly. Imitating supposedly, according to her, of course; that's all exactly!, Silvao LUCINDAÇIO. Which one was doing so, the same."

"Irene Lucindaçio dragging, dragging and dragging; Irene Lucindaçio dragging, dragging and dragging, ridiculously home or elsewhere; dragging and dragging, ridiculously home or elsewhere! That's all: Dragging and dragging, ridiculously home or elsewhere!, whatever. Imitating supposedly, according to her, of course; that's all agreed!, Amy Sophia LEBRETONA. Which one was doing so, the same."

"Irene Lucindaçio walked decidedly it easy, take it easy, take it easy; walked decidedly it easy, take it easy, take it easy! That's all: walked decidedly it easy, take it easy, take it easy!; imitating supposedly, according to her, of course; that's all righto!, Elisio Gomez Rodriguez. Which one was doing so, the same."

"Irene Lucindaçio walked sweet, sweet, sweetly; walked sweet, sweet, sweetly! That's all: Walked sweet, sweet, sweetly!; imitating supposedly, according to her, of course; that's all uh – huh!, Adelino JACINTA. Which one was doing so, the same."

"Irene Lucindaçio decidedly walked slowly; decidedly walked slowly! That's all: Decidedly walked slowly!; imitating supposedly, according to her, of course; that's all aye!, Eliodoro RODRIGUEZ. Which one was doing so, the same."

"Irene Lucindaçio walked same excruciatingly now; walked same excruciatingly now! That's all: Walked same excruciatingly now. Imitating supposedly, according to her, of course; that's all aye – aye!, Lopez Ramiro."

"Her heart was beating, beating, beating fast; was beating, beating, beating fast! That's all: Was beating, beating, beating fast!, and improperly ("improperly"; "improperly"! That's all: "Improperly"!, [so that did not suit]; imitating supposedly, according to her, of course; that's all OK!, Alberto Rodriguez). Which one was doing so, the same."

"Irene Lucindaçio bowed, saluted, bowed politely; bowed, saluted, bowed politely! That's all: Bowed, saluted, bowed politely!, and ridiculously vacuum; ridiculously vacuum! That's all: ridiculously vacuum!; there were people she had known before, who had come to visit her; imitating supposedly, according to her, of course; that's: Oll: Uh – huhl, Ma'am RAPHAËL RAFAI A Which one was doing so, the same."

"but that people unfortunately, alas!, the other people who know the knowing (; knowing her Irene Lucindaçio) had consequently not only never and never, never; and never, never; and never, never; and never, never, ever seen before; but also that, even at times then 'that Irene greet them; imitating supposedly, according to her, of course; that's all yeah!, The Reverend Pastor Augy Wucher. Which one was doing so, the same."

"Irene Lucindaçio would there often enough, only welcome a vacuum; and this, with all the most distinguished possible bows; with all the most distinguished possible bows! That's all: With all the most distinguished possible bows!; imitating supposedly, according to her, of course; that's all Okay!, Ernesto DOMINGUEZ ALMEIDA. Which one was doing so, the same."

"like the bows of which are exhibited vis-à-vis the Kings or Queens, for example). Imitating supposedly, according to her, of course; of course! That's all: Of course!, Marta VITALINO. Imitating supposedly, according to her, of course; obviously! That's all: Obviously!, Barrene LUCINDAÇIO. Which one was doing so, the same."

"Once: Irene Lucindaçio was said very explicitly, be normal. In other words: Irene Lucindaçio would say owning her mind in very; very, very well! That's all: Very, very well!; very, very good condition; and therefore Irene Lucindaçio systematically; *systematically! That's all: Systematically!,* will refuse any help that they were trying to bring to her. Imitating supposedly, according to her, of course; verily! That's all verily!, Aziz OLENGA. Which one was doing so, the same."

"Another blow: Irene Lucindaçio eventually recognize:" That, Irene Lucindaçio was not Irene Lucindaçio herself." Imitating supposedly, according to her, of course; very well! That's all:

Very well!, Fren Teach Montgo. Which one was doing so, the same."

"Irene Lucindaçio eventually recognize: "That, Irene Lucindaçio would become "remained"; that, Irene Lucindaçio would become "remained"; that's all: That, Irene Lucindaçio would become "remained". "Imitating supposedly, according to her, of course; surely! That's all surely!, Bernadette Of The Sister Rosalie. Which one was doing so, the same."

"Irene Lucindaçio eventually, recognize: "That, Irene Lucindaçio would become "mentally retarded"; that, Irene Lucindaçio would become "remained"; that's all: That, Irene Lucindaçio would become "remained". Imitating supposedly, according to her, of course; that's all indeed!, agreed!, José Manuel GLORIA." Imitating supposedly, according to her, of course; of course! That's all: Of course!, Aminata Ayichatoune. Which one was doing so, the same."

"Irene Lucindaçio eventually recognize: "That, Irene Lucindaçio would become "siphoned off"; that, Irene Lucindaçio would become "siphoned off"! That's all: That, Irene Lucindaçio would become "siphoned off". Imitating supposedly, according to her, of course; that's all agreed!, indeed!, Camilo CARVALHO. Which one was doing so, the same.""

"Irene Lucindaçio would simply become "thin-skinned"; would simply become "thin-skinned"! That's all: Would simply become "thin-skinned". And without the neuropsychological care; without the neuropsychological care! That's all: Without the neuropsychological care!, the delirium tremens of Irene Lucindaçio had simply multiplied over and over. And again and again. And yes ih! Of course! Absolutely! That's all absolutely!, Imitating supposedly, according to her, of course; certainly! That's all: Certainly!, Claudio CAETANO. Which one was doing so, the same."... / ...!"".

.../... And MAMPUYA Sings and Dances
of the Samba. DRAWING:

Indeed, agreed: Isaac To Waddle
and To Drum on MAMPUYA;
and MAMPUYA Sings and Dances of
the Samba. DEMONSTRATION:

"NOTHING DO WOULD GO MORE
BETWEEN ALBERTO RODRIGUEZ AND THAT
WHICH THE DESTINY HAD PROMOTED
AND ENCOURAGED HIM THE MEETING;
THAT IS TO SAY: "IRENE LUCINDAÇIO OF
REAR - OFFSPRING CONGOLESE.""

In this New Episode (as always and always again) "BaLiSambaSty" or "the Literary Walk in Samba – Style" goes so far to assert with all its Cruise style. Demonstration:

7. – "IRENE AND AN OTHER FORM OF TORTURE OF HER OWN CONSCIENCE". (CONTINUATION).

Preceded by:

6. – "Irene LUCINDAÇIO, the daughter of Jupiter and Aphrodite". (CONTINUATION).

and:

7. – "IRENE AND AN OTHER FORM OF TORTURE OF HER OWN CONSCIENCE". (BEGINNING).

And in this Episode – again and again and again and again, we are going between – others to face at ONE PARA – NORMAL TO THE SUPERLATIVE RELATIVE FOR ALL THE LIFE OF ALL THE DAYS AND AROUND THE WORLD, leading by ITS SUPERNATURAL AND ITS MYSTERY OF THE UNIVERSE, of course: Of course! That's all: Of course!, THE EMOTIONAL DISORDER PSYCHOSOMATIC; or to better express it, causing: THE PSYCHIC EMOI. It's really all A SPOOKY STORY as one: the Writer Isaac MAMPUYA Samba alone likes recounting it.

The French Act of 11 March 1957 authorizing, under paragraphs 2 and 3 of Article 41, on the one hand, that "copies or reproductions strictly reserved for private use and not intended for collective use "and, secondly, analyses and short quotations for the purposes of example and illustration," any reproduction or integral or partial reproduction without the consent of the author or his heirs or assigns, is unlawful "(paragraph 1 of Article 40).

This representation or reproduction, by any means whatsoever, constitutes an infringement punishable by Articles 425 and following of the Penal Code.

PRINCIPLE

"The Imaginary" first;

   then "(1) {*"The Real" truth "of the Past"; but "transplanted",
so to speak.*} the Real " after that."

SUMMARY

As the football players for example dribble with the ball; and it turns out that, the Author Isaac MAMPUYA Samba as for him with his Scripture, he simply dribbles with: 26 Letters of Phoenician Alphabet; 10 Numbers of Arabic Numeral and a Pencil or a Computer; with above all to crown the whole, the ZEST: Effective Innate Personal Talent. And so, always and always generating for Isaac MAMPUYA Samba, an Unique Scripture; or rather: And so, always and always generating for IsMaSa, an Unique Scripture to the Superlative; or, in order to be able to express it, one could not do better: And so, always and always generating for Isaac MAMPUYA Samba, an Unique Scripture in the Superlative of the Superlatives. And as a result, the Tour is automatically played: The Notoriety; a Planetary Notoriety that happens or rather: which is confirmed.

Demonstration: ".../...".

Signed: IsMaSa.

Isaac MAMPUYA Samba owns the Scripture for sale; or rather, he has the Scripture to spare; or in order to be able to express it much more explicitly: Isaac MAMPUYA Samba is the synonym – even of the Quiet Force in Strong Scripture. Drawing .../...

NOTE

"INVISIBLE WRITING"

"**A**ccording to "Le Petit Larousse", "A Reflection" is"

"among others: "The action of the mind that thinks,"

"which examines and compares his thoughts; resulting judgment.","

"This one is then read "The Reflection" following about a certain "it".""

"**H**e "written, but alas!, unfortunately,"

"nobody could really understand "him";"

"in order for to not let downright heard;"

or rather systematically e.g."

"that "Nobody could" "understanding "him" at all, at all."

"And for good reason? "He" aims hardly "the Intellect of the people";"

"but rather "their Conscientiousness"."

""He" does not include "Mind";"

"but rather "The Interior Judgement on the Moral Quality"

"of an act; or act to ask. "."

"In short, "There" is not at all, at all, this body"

"Anatomical called "Brain" so to speak;"

"but rather, that other body [always Anatomically"

"indeed]; but nevertheless, nevertheless! That's all: Nevertheless!, called "Heart"."

"To understand this, "He" in question, in fact"

"we should not be regarded primarily developed at the forefront"

"the writings lines; but rather "the between-the-lines "; or to better express it:"

"We should absolutely necessary to consider in the first"

"Plan: "The Invisible Writings lines " hiding"

"between the lines of "this present little text"."

"And that "He" in question, with such writing,"

   "that is, "He", the "Being" – There?"

"This "He" is "X"?"

"This "He" is "Y"?"

"And who he is, this "X" -There?"

"And who he is, this "Y" -There? ".

"Is – "He" the Writer Is Ma Sa or the Famous Author Isaac MAMPUYA Samba?"

"Unquestionably, it absolutely cans only be the Him, himself."».

Signed Reflection: Is Ma Sa

or Isaac MAMPUYA Samba.

"Certainly; certainly! That's all: Certainly!, it is wrong, for such acts … / … But "the poor" … / … rather needs "psychic" care, not to say "mental!"; that "a prison incarceration»! From where … / ….".

But during that time, Alberto Rodriguez remained "rot" in prison of WORMWOOD SCRUBS (at Wormwood Street in the eastern part of the British capital). Indeed, that's all indeed!, agreed!, the new appointment was expected in "two weeks"; we did not even slow on the back of it. They had simply said: "Whether we will review his case again in six months.".

Why

It was: "Because it took absolutely; absolutely! That's all absolutely!, punishing; as he had in himself, no less committed several serious crimes, among others, "the plot" or "conspiracy" and "perjury"."

It is finally decided, after, in all, a year and a half in prison; we would ruthlessly suppress the young Alberto Rodriguez at his home in Sao Paulo, despite its "NINE YEARS" finally, past in Britain.

But only one his Lawyer Mistress Alcina BARBARA (1) { : *Although Mistress Alcina BARBARA was chosen to defend Alberto Rodriguez, for the Services of Help Jurisdictional; it is because: that one, was in the very, verily! That's all verily!, difficult situation in which he apparently found; he could hardly afford to pay "fees" of pleading.* } had not dropped at all. Try it to nullify the threat of expulsion and referral RODRIGUEZ on his release from prison, to his home in São Paulo; and that, inexorably; for someone who had finally, spent NINE YEARS in England; and which previously had the Status of a foreign student in this country; and that since he had found himself in an irregular situation; that is to say, without a residence permit.

In order to achieve this, Mistress Alcina BARBARA (2) { : *His Lawyer.* }, would "play" the fact: "It is there, someone who "had not only spent many years in our country. (3) { : *Looks like it.* } " ; "but, it is there, someone who is the father of a little girl who had legally obtained the British nationality, by the fact of her birth, on this country. (4). { : Would add Mistress Alcina BARBARA. ". }".

For Mistress Alcina BARBARA: "There [was] therefore hunt "the father of a British child". However, the latter would naturally need her father, as for almost the other children of the world."

In the meantime; that is to say, during the time that Rodriguez would continue to serve his sentence in prison [and for good reason], the IRENE friends, and even some friends and cousins of RODRIGUEZ, no longer would stop at all to say that:

" ... / ... Anyway, Alberto Rodriguez was "a misanthrope wizard"; a sadistic formidable; "a jealous devil"; very jealous; very; verily! That's all verily!, very jealous; an evil; and a madman. He was a criminal who had committed crimes beyond belief, as he had:

not only severely beaten "the shepherdess", to the point of sending in intensive care at the hospital;

not only that he did not hesitate for a little while, to bully children thereof, including "its own smaller girl Elisio RODRIGUEZ GOMEZ"; which did not come then, to be born "there were exactly; exactly! That's all exactly!, ten months", at that time;

not only that he had even beaten, ERNESTO, his son of ten years;

but he did not at all, at all, hesitate a little while, to send wrong (5) { : *Following a visceral jealousy; dangerous; and blind.* } "in jail", that one, he was yet "very; very; verily! That's all verily!, very madly in love".

They continued: "Alberto Rodriguez had committed such a heinous crime; or rather of such heinous crimes; Machiavellian; heinous and deplorable! So he deserves great, and exit from prison, he is returned to his home in São Paulo, as a simple ordinary parcel of post."

On balance, Miss Irene LUCINDAÇIO also shared this opinion very well. Very well! That's all: Very well! Even her cousin João – Santos BARRAY; which was during the time that Irene had been locked, occupied "the housing two pieces" of the latter; so that its owner does not recover; otherwise, the output of IRENE, the process in order to be able to recover her children would be severely compromised; this João – Santos BARRAY also shared the opinion of those people.

Alberto Rodriguez for his part, he would be informed about all these noises that "took place" outside the prison environment; and this: about him and to his detriment; through the correspondence more or less regularly, that he maintained, with some of his other faithful friends, among others: Guy Ammar; Robert MERYC; and Morris HAMILTON. That said, from his cell, ALBERTO threaten Irene LUCINDAÇIO by successive letters, like what, that: as long as it still occupy, for example, "this two – room house" that he had succeeded for rent, though it was in the name of her (6) { : *That is to say: "his Archduchess"; little to say for example "his ex- Duchess".* }; he would continue therefore to piss very seriously on her.

In turn the children, initially, they were always kept by the "EWO / ESW"; the "L E" and "A C".

That was why so?

It was precisely the fact of the request, Miss Irene LUCINDAÇIO; it is because the latter had (7) { : *During this time, very precisely.* } found a job as "cleaning woman" in one of the buildings of the "Company British Air Way", with hourly from Monday to Friday from 06: 30 to 10 30 H; then 16: 30 ', 20 30 H' (8). { : *That is to say, "eight full hours" a day.* }. And consequently; *and consequently! That's all: And consequently!,* it was not any time to take care of her two kids (9). { : *In order to wake them up around 07 H 10; because at that time, it would be a party to his work as "cleaning woman" to "British Air Way".* }. Then: to give them very verily! That's all verily!, quickly: their breakfast; to dress; to bring them in elementary school [ERNESTO the eldest son of IRENE, had many delays because of the language; that was why he was still in primary school]; and bring the younger [that is to say: ELISIO], in the Nursery. Then, in the evening around 16: 30 ' – 18 H 00': retrieve them; whereas at that time, she still found her work; so there! Hence, she had herself (10) { : *Deliberately.* } preferred to let hers kids still available to "EWO / ESW"; the "L E" and "A C"; "then later (1) { : *She did not know exactly; exactly! That's all exactly!, when yet thick; so really: She did not know yet exactly when. }*, we would see: what we could do so! " (2). { *: Looks like she finally, thinks in the bottom of herself. }*.

On Side "residence permit", Miss Irene LUCINDACIO always had a provisional receipt; renewable; no problem; every six months [it was something!]. Master Gamal CHAUVRY; the Lawyer who had dealt with the case of IRENE; although he too was only named by the Jurisdictional Assistance Services (3) { *: This is because "these two antagonistic" to the point where they were, "apparently" they could not even afford "luxury" to go get everyone (that is, saying each "antagonistic", or to put it differently: Alberto Rodriguez and Irene LUCINDAÇIO): a Lawyer. That was why they had been assisted by the Lawyers chosen beforehand by the Jurisdictional Assistance Services. }*; he had (4) { *: As also the Lawyer of Alberto RODRIGUEZ; that is to say: Mistress Alcina BARBARA, was it. }* advocated the fate of "his client" Irene LUCINDAÇIO with all "his soul and all his conscience";

or to be able to put it on another way: "with all his devotion". Thus, it would still be up to speed the regularly, decisions that are going to take, in respect of Alberto RODRIGUEZ; and he also said regularly in his "former client"; that is to say, to Miss Irene LUCINDAÇIO.

It would be thus, that only two months before the end of the prison of RODRIGUEZ; IRENE will know already, that Alberto Rodriguez just, would inexorably return at his home in Sao

Paulo; so that the Brazilian authorities still hold once again, his case on the spot in their country; that is to say: Brazil.

But as his Lawyer, Mistress Alcina BARBARA wanted to make every effort in order to bring out "her client Alberto Rodriguez" in "this dirty mess"; in which he found himself; she advanced again, "the argument" that, which was: "... / ... Therefore, "chase" the father of a young British", "by birth"; and that we had no right to do so! ... / ...!".

This argument as such, was "hardly" unwound foundation. It was even more than enough to demand that the sentence that the young Alberto Rodriguez had had to serve in the British prison cells, was sufficient about it! And therefore, its release of "metal", we should not only stop the deportation process against him but, we should also regularize undoubtedly; undoubtedly! That's all: Undoubtedly!, his residency Status.

"After all, had he not finally, passed a decade or so in England?

Was he not the father of a little British, recognized as such by "birth"?

Or rather, for "her birth on British soil"? (5) ". { : *Asked "Mistress" (or rather the Lawyer) Alcina BARBARA; (that is to say, the Lawyer of Alberto Rodriguez); she would ask it, to "the Public Ministry".* }.

The arguments advanced by Mistress Alcina BARBARA, being size, the Crown could not see at all:

How stuck Alberto RODRIGUEZ.

Since even for this case of "cocaine", nothing was really sure, surely! That's all surely!, to everyone that this was Alberto Rodriguez himself, really "a dealer".

There arose after all, this question is because we could not at all understand this, that: –––".

"Without anything! Without being spun, for example, the anti – stunning – brigade, and that one can go to denounce, as himself, in good faith! And that, for a case of resale of drugs! "For all to see": ––– ".

"Neither one; that is to say: Irene LUCINDAÇIO; or the other; that is to say: Alberto Rodriguez, was ultimately "a dealer".

"With so concerned the presence of "the cocaine"; which was intended to arrest Miss IRENE, we concluded only:

"... / ... Alberto RODRIGUEZ was perhaps become a little consumer "of the thing"! If we were having to "lock" for example all small consumers, it would inevitably First, start by building, "twenty times" more prison places! ".

"But as to the fact that A. RODRIGUEZ was heavily abused: and "his children"; and his "Salome IRENE"; so much so, that he even "accidentally" sent her, to the hospital; Mistress Alcina BARBARA, had asked the prosecution and "the members of the jury" that: –––" .

"Certainly, certainly! That's all: Certainly!, it is wrong, of such actions!".

"Certainly, certainly! That's all: Certainly!, slippages such domestic scenes, are not tolerable!".

"**B**ut "the poor" Alberto Rodriguez is he finally, became a little bit, in reality no more; no less: like a neurotic depressive; which rather needs "the psychics care"; for not to say: "the psychiatric care"; that "a prison incarceration"?

"This raises the question: Is it normal to deny for him, these therapeutics care; and instead, to "punish him" severely?"

"For Mistress BARBARA: "These domestic scenes had slipped; This is simply because "the guy" likes jealously; or very, verily! That's all verily!, jealously, "his girlfriend"! Hence, the question: He who loves "very, verily! That's all verily!, closely" "the beauty", he absolutely; absolutely! That's all absolutely!, deserves to be "severely punished" for "this act of love"?

Considering all these arguments from Mistress Alcina BARBARA, the question, as to the output of the prison RODRIGUEZ, that it remains in Britain, no longer pose a problem at all.

One only needed; and this, of course: Of course! That's all: Of course!, urgently (; "urgently", that is to say, within a short time only: four days), the Two Official Documents:

A Timed Birth of the children Elisio RODRIGUEZ GOMEZ; that is to say, the girl of A. RODRIGUEZ; which was born when the latter was in "jail" for the first time; and that, for a period of ten months.

And then saw Alberto Rodriguez and Irene LUCINDAÇIO were not "married"; and they were then, that living "conjugal relationship", waiting perhaps, "a possible marriage"; which can be further delay would not; if and only if there were no major disagreements between "the two persons"; then we had urgently also (6) { : *[And that, absolutely; absolutely! That's all absolutely!].* } needs "a Certificate of Recognition of the child by the father (7) " { : *That is to say: Alberto Rodriguez established by the City Council of their shared "Certificate".* }, to really confirm that:

> not only Alberto Rodriguez was actually the father of "a little British boy"; or rather, a little British girl;

> not only that one, had indeed; that's all indeed!, agreed!, recognized his child by an Official Act;

> but consequently, it [the female child] was absolutely; absolutely! That's all absolutely!, needs her father in order to help her also, to her education.

They said, things seemed to settle for Alberto Rodriguez, Legally speaking.

$\mathbf{B}$ut alas!, unfortunately; unfortunately, alas! That's all: Unfortunately, alas!, when Legally speaking, the things seemed to settle for "the poor" Alberto RODRIGUEZ!; they would lock "tightly and mercilessly" by the unwillingness of Miss Irene LUCINDAÇIO herself; which, thinking about all the injustices that she had, had to know; and including this one exactly, exactly! That's all exactly!, was the instigator; that is to say, thinking of the fact that she was trapped, because of "an informer" who had no sense of being; because "the charge" which indeed; that's all agreed!, indeed!, it does was yet to anything in this she was accused unjustly; then, the things would block because of Irene LUCINDAÇIO precisely; very, verily! That's all verily!, categorically deny that therefore, to send within the time provided for this purpose, before the judge, the Papers and requested emergency.

Alberto RODRIGUEZ respect to him, it was right after the last of the last pleading of "Mistress" Alcina BARBARA, released from prison in WORMWOOD SCRUBS; and he was then taken and kept in a Police Station; the Police Station "R. Neville" (or rather: the Police Station "The King maker" ["The King Maker"]), meanwhile, within four business days, so that we do reach the State Civil Acts, Original; which had been requested; or failing originals; then their Certified and True Copies; or else: Simply Duplicates. Hence, the fact that this period of "Four days" (we did not take into account the days of weekends and holidays). Hence the fact that this period of "Four days", was actually even too, if and only if it were accepted quite frankly, to get him; and then to send to him, in because these Papers Marital Status.

In the event that, within that period, in principle, very, verily! That's all verily!, ample, they were hardly reached the Commissioner; we would simply proceed with the expulsion of the person concerned; that is to say: RODRIGUEZ, to send him home in Sao Paulo.

In this Police Station, everyone who was in custody, there was only "one inmate", supposed to be "deportable" and deported for that time, precisely; *precisely! That's all: Precisely!;* and he was Alberto RODRIGUEZ.

When the latter is still found in the Commissioner, pending us to send the Papers that had been claimed; from the very, verily! That's all verily!, first night he had already sought permission from the "Brigadier Chief"; which was called Gerald FRANCK so he cans join his "calf IRENE", by telephone.

He had indeed; that's all indeed!, agreed!, allowed joining it.

But only here, it would not happen at all, at all, to reach precisely; or rather, to put it more correctly: this one in question, did not want at all, at all feel; and consequently; *and consequently! That's all: And consequently!,* she had always and still always hung up; even from the moment she heard only his voice.

With the authorization of the Officers on duty, Rodriguez did in all, several attempts; but unfortunately alas!; *unfortunately, alas! That's all: Unfortunately, alas!,* every time, it was the same thing: Irene LUCINDAÇIO was up at all, at all to speak to him; and she was really very, verily! That's all verily!, very, very firm in her decision. It was very, verily! That's all verily!, very, very, very adamant; and Alberto Rodriguez was stuck net. He had tried everything twelve times. But nothing to do, he did not succeed therein. He hardly managed to contact Miss Irene LUCINDAÇIO.

However, he had no other alternative, that: to abandon that path.

There was no other alternately as: to abandon that path which was to come into direct contact with that one. Hence the fact, so much that he found himself in the imminent need; then the idea came to him in his head to go through a third party; which surely, surely! That's all surely!, very, very succeed in not getting hung up.

" ... / ... Tell her very explicitly; explicitly! That's all: Explicitly!, and repeats it to her, that the unpardonable sin; which fault was the basis of all this "degeneration" was committed by the blind "a guy"and not experienced for "hymen life"! ... / ....".

That said, the small time of "Four days", spun into full speed; and it was absolutely; absolutely! That's all absolutely!, a solution to save the plight of Alberto Rodriguez. In doing so, he had thought about making one last attempt, passing two phone calls, one of which, the Intelligence Service, to request the telephone number of one of his true friends 1 { *: [This is to say, a certain Robert MERYC].* }; which phone number of one of his true friends just 1 ; and yet which, until then, he still remembered and still always by heart; but curiously; curiously! That's all: Curiously!, during that moment precisely which he desperately needed it, he did not remember it just, at all, at all. He could not even remember any more, if at all, for example: the number was on the red list or not. What sacred memory hole!

That said, the small time of "Four days," always spun and still always in full speed; and there remained but "Two" (; more than "two days", since it hardly counts weekends and holidays, for the administration, as did most of activities, are closed on these days, so it's hard to pick up the State – Civil Papers, in the District Offices, which are obviously; obviously! That's all: Obviously!, closed).

That said, Rodriguez still had a 2 { : *In the early evening; that is to say, two days after he made the first attempt to call to herself, Miss Irene LUCINDAÇIO.* } night asked permission from the Officer Gerald FRANCK; which was, together with some of his colleagues, custody, that evening, to spend another two last calls.

The Officer being kind; even very kind to him; he said: "Go in this room there, behind you, right at the entrance; just out the door, on the left, there is a wall phone. Lift the handset; and make the code number "0 – 0"; to exit from the Site."

A. RODRIGUEZ: "Thank you very much! You are really nice, "Sir" the Officer."

"Sir" the Officer Gerald FRENNK: "Be more or less short anyway huh!, young man! That's all OK!".

A. RODRIGUEZ: "Okay. That's all Okay!".

And Alberto Rodriguez had initially phoned the Intelligence Services. And as his friend Robert MERYC is not included on the Red List; so, he managed to get the number of the latter, to whom he was going to send a very, verily! That's all verily!, very, very urgent message to "his Eva, IRENE", if not "his ex – Calf". By calling ROBERT, RODRIGUEZ had fallen on "the Delilah" of the latter, by the name of Karen Hamel, wife MERYC; and he said: "Hello! This is me RODRIGUEZ! Alberto RODRIGUEZ!".

Karen HAMEL, wife MERYC: "Ah! Hello Alberto RODRIGUEZ!"

RODRIGUEZ: "Hello Karen!"

Karen: "Oh!, you're out of "jail"? Where are you now?"

RODRIGUEZ: "Karen, I do not have much time! Does "your Adam ROBERT" is there? I really want to talk to him; and it's really very, verily! That's all verily!, very, very urgent!"

Karen: "You're lucky RODRIGUEZ! ROBERT has arrived just as it is 18 hours; and he often comes home from his work at that time here! Hold on, I'll call him for you!".

Karen, addressing to her "hominid ROBERT": "ROBERT! Come quickly! This is from RODRIGUEZ! He is already out of jail! He absolutely; absolutely! That's all absolutely!, wants to talk to you! And he says it's really, really urgent!".

Robert MERYC, to Alberto Rodriguez: "Oh!, hello RODRIGUEZ! That's it! You came out now? What good news!".

RODRIGUEZ: "Actually my dear friend Robert MERYC! I'm not at all out! There is a big problem! ... / ...!".

Alberto Rodriguez had devised a strategy very lives, he thought: ""If it could work"! "His former beloved" IRENE would anyway end up having "tender heart"; that is to say, she would anyway end up having pity on him; and therefore she would eventually take steps in order to submit those Papers required urgently.". RODRIGUEZ not especially wanted to express all very explicitly; explicitly! That's all: Explicitly!, to his friend Robert MERYC that: when we Officially establish "the authorship" that existed between himself Alberto RODRIGUEZ on the one hand; and on the other hand, Elisio RODRIGUEZ GOMEZ, "the little British girl by the Law of the ground"; or "birth right"; would be allowed without further ado more.

For this, A. Rodriguez would tell to Robert MERYC: "... / ... ROBERT! There is a big problem! I am not yet released! I actually got out of the prison of WORMWOOD SCRUBS as such! But just now, I am kept in Police custody in a Police Station! I am condemned to deportation, in arriving at my home in Sao Paulo, in at all now: "Forty eight hours flat so to speak, exactly! Exactly! That's all exactly! ".

"The Officer Gerard FRANCK here has given me just a few minutes of authorization to use their wall telephone device; and that's it, I'm calling you!

You do not believe in your ears my friend ROBERT; but it's true! And what is true? What is true, that: Oddly, I could not remember even not at all, at all, your phone number! And I was forced to call first, the Service of Information!

They said, in any case, "in at all now: Forty eight hours flat as it exactly", exactly! That's all exactly!, I will take the plane "forcibly" in order to return home to Sao Paulo!

That's all my time as a Lawyer, Mistress Alcina BARBARA was able, despite all her efforts without slightest gently in my favour; it's like being time she could snatch despite it; and this call; it's a time she could, despite it getting time to just to Irene, can do anyway proof of humanism to me; that is to say, for her to do what is necessary, so that the paternity between me and the child Elisio RODRIGUEZ GOMEZ we actually establish!

For this, we need Acts of Civil Status 3.

{ : "Originals or Copies or Duplicates" ["Photocopies"], whatever! But in the case of the latter, it will be just "Copy" or "Copies" Certified and Conformity "of Sanctimonious" and asked anyway. }. We really need the Birth Certificate and the "Certificate of Recognition of the child", we did establish by myself and her, IRENE, at City Hall already once (1). { : Said Alberto Rodriguez, on the phone to his friend Robert MERYC. }."It was absolutely;

Absolutely! That's all absolutely!, need these "Palpable - there" – Officials Proofs: cause, to approve the Paternity between me and the child ELISIO verbally "does indeed; that's all agreed!, indeed!, pose [and they have also reason to stress], no serious credit!". This is because after all, everyone would say something like: "Ah!, I too am the father of so and so! (2) ". { : *Looks RODRIGUEZ then.* }."

"The one that I would present "the Papers" requested, it is because I, as such; as you also know very, very; very, very well! That's all: Very, very well!, with Karen ("your Beauty!"). This is because myself, I have more Papers to stay, in rules! I'm at the Police Station; and it did not give me too much, too much time to call! Hence, you who are a great friend of mine; and you know it very, very; very, very well! That's all: Very, very well!; our phone number by heart! And if in case [not impossible elsewhere], where you will remind you more of this issue! I am reminding it to you! """

ROBERT: "I still have in my notebook. Wait a second. Is not that it is: 7 – 6 – 5 – 4 – 3 – 2 – 1 – 0?"

RODRIGUEZ:"Yeah! That's: Oll Korrect!, it is that! A fairly easy to remember number; because it is sufficient to decrease the numbers, from: 7 to 0! So call me for this IRENE! And tries to persuade her to do anyway a gesture, in order to "liberate her own personal conscience"; ROBERT trying to do this for me please! Be my way; this is because the Commissioner's goodwill, let me call, but said to me, whether I am anyway, more or less short! Hence, they allowed me; but we should not either, I took the opportunity to abuse it too! There are two days, they are very, verily! That's all verily!, nice, the Officers on duty, had allowed me to call."

"But I had two days previously (3) { : "[48 hours], to fully specify". Looks like Alberto RODRIGUEZ. }, previously! That's all: Previously!, attempted to call myself IRENE and try to talk to her what I have to say it! But each time, when I call, I come, right now, she hangs up on me! Each time I call her, from herself, she only hears my voice without even giving me the time to introduce myself; she hangs up on me in the nose!"

"So in this situation, it is impossible to talk to her! Since this is from "twenty four hours", "twelve times in a row", she hangs up the phone to me on the nose! (4) { : "Hence, on average, once every two hours". Then says RODRIGUEZ. };"

""That is why my friend Robert! Try talking to her, from me!""

""Tell to her clearly; clearly! That's all: clearly explicitly!, that it does not matter that we start living together again; since I know very well; very well! That's all: Very well!, that this would interest never, ever, never, ever; and never, ever, never, ever! And I know definitely very, very good! Very, very well! That's all: Very, very well!""

""Tell to her clearly; clearly! That's all: clearly explicitly!, that it does not matter that I RODRIGUEZ, I will come out soon; and I would still occupy the house; which, though praised in her name; but nevertheless; *nevertheless! That's all: Nevertheless!,* it was me Alberto Rodriguez, who had gotten it!""

""Tell to her clearly; clearly! That's all: clearly explicitly!, that it does not matter, I will once again show to her, this visceral, exacerbated and dangerous jealousy; that I have often used, to make to her a sad demonstration; and I recognize it myself.""

""Tell to her clearly; clearly! That's all: clearly explicitly!, to be truly free to lead her life as she hears the lead; even with Lopez Ramiro, for example! And it is now well and truly a bargain!""

"Specifies to her clearly; clearly! That's all: clearly explicitly!, that she is now free to live life as she wants; among others, "to go with any kind as she hears just to do it!". It is indeed; that's all agreed!, indeed!, now, her own business!"

"Tell to her clearly, clearly! That's all: clearly explicitly!, I let her finally (5) { : *"Above all it is rented in her name", would clarify to her, "the expelled Alberto Rodriguez". Note that everyone was saying it, were more or less listened carefully by some Officers; who were on duty that night; which the left call for more or less long.* }, she occupies the cockpit! Although in reality it was me RODRIGUEZ who had gotten it; and though there was not long ago, I threatened her by various successive and repeated letters, I did send to her from the prison; and which were also remained "the dead letters"; that if I went out one day (as it would have been necessary for me to finish it anyway, for sure, surely! That's all surely!, a good day out for these crimes I had committed); that: as long as it still occupy the apartment, she would suffer (6)!

{ : "I always should piss off undoubtedly! That's all: Undoubtedly!, very seriously: "I wrote to her several times in my mail; which remained alas!, unfortunately, as only "the dead letters". ", Alberto Rodriguez would say to him Robert MERYC, in that long phone conversation. }."

"Tell her very clearly, clearly! That's all: clearly explicitly!, that I abandon for her now; and that finally, this house, where she also currently lives with one of his cousins (7) *{ : That is to say: João – Santos BARRAY. }*; I would rather say, with one of her lovers, who just arrived, there is a little more than a year only, from Portugal, or better said, from Madeira Islands (8)! *{ : "And as I RODRIGUEZ, I know; since one had written it to me; this is because, in any case, IRENE, as I know her, she could not stay without "lover" eventually; especially that, she is "very, very; very, very well! That's all: Very, very well!, beautiful", "after all!", RODRIGUEZ would continue. }."*

"Tell to her very clearly, very clearly! That's all: very clearly explicitly!, that I give her all the chattels that I had paid; and which are located in "this home"; where she lives (9)! *{ : Would say RODRIGUEZ, at ROBERT thereafter. }."*

"Tell to her very explicitly; very explicitly! That's all: Very explicitly!, and repeats it to her, that the unpardonable sin (10) *{ : "What I have committed", would say RODRIGUEZ, at his* *friend Robert, on the phone.* }; which fault was the basis of any "degeneration" was committed by the blind; by "a Son of Adam" not experienced in marital life! And "this Sparrow" is who? And "this Bird", is me Alberto Rodriguez, the only son of Eliodoro RODRIGUEZ and Adelina JACINTA.!"" ... / ... "."

CHAPTER: III

"... / ... Tell to her clearly! That's all: clearly explicitly!, that I had crossed the line, it's because I had loved her and elsewhere about it, I still love her forever; and I wanted to keep to myself and not share her, with some Lopez Ramiro!".

The Officer Gerald FRANCK, after listening to some "beautiful love sentences" imposed by "the expelled; that is to say", by Alberto Rodriguez; he could not help saying to his colleague for example Bruno GRANDA; which was like him, also on duty that day: "Eh!, eh BRUNO?"

Bruno GRANDA: "Yeah! That's all correct!, ih!, ih, ih!"

Gerald FRANCK: "Hear therefore "the beautiful words of love" of the "expelled"; and watch very, very; very, very well! That's all: Very, very well!, quietly at the same time, their exposed emotions!"

Bruno GRANDA: "Where".

Gerald FRANCK: "In wall then phone! But pretend not to look at him; while watching quietly enough! And listen to, at the same time all those he tells to his interlocutor!".

Bruno GRANDA: "Or I listen at the same time, all those he tells to his interlocutor! You never know eh!".

Gerald FRANCK: "I say, "the speaker"; this is because he mentioned the first name of his friend in question, being on the phone; and the first name just, is ROBERT!"

Bruno GRANDA: "Yep! That's all affirmative!, in this case "contact" then!".

Gerald FRANCK: "Listen: How he described how he had loved "some chick"!"

Bruno GRANDA: "Okay! That's all absolutely!, Let's hear it!".

Gerald FRANCK: "OK! That's all exactly!, Let's hear it!".

And Alberto Rodriguez kept talking to his friend Robert MERYC, at the phone of the Police Station.

RODRIGUEZ, to ROBERT: ""Tell to her, very clearly; clearly! That's all: clearly explicitly!, and repeat it to her, that I RODRIGUEZ, the unforgivable fault that I had committed; this misconduct, appears to be that of love "a Countess", in this case, her, Irene

LUCINDAÇIO more than any other living being in this world; including more than myself!"

Bruno GRANDA, speaking to his colleague Gerald FRANCK: "Oh!, there! How beautiful! Wait, hold out, hold out FRANCK! I'm going to call "our colleague female cop" Joanna EDITH, for it also, that she comes listen to these lovely romantic phrases! And we will see what her reaction would be, as "a female being" exactly! Exactly! That's all exactly!".

Gerald FRANCK: "Go! Call her. As she is a "lady"; she will give us a review!".

Bruno GRANDA: "Good! It certainly; certainly! That's all: Certainly!, should not interrupt eh!"

Gerald FRANCK: "Do not worry BRUNO! Do not worry!"

And Ma'am Joanna EDITH arrived; and she listened together with hers two colleagues: Gerald FRANCK and Bruno GRANDA; and that, very, verily! That's all verily!, quietly, they said that the "expelled" Alberto RODRIGUEZ.

That said, Ma'am Edith would say: "How beautifull Do not interrupt, to listen more, these beautiful words of love!"

Gerald FRANCK: "Certainly; certainly; certainly! That's all: Certainly!, that "expelled" misadventures a little bit, too much with the telephone! But I let him go even a little while; and as you will continue to listen to his fine words! But more or less discreetly; otherwise, if he finds out what he's like watching and listening; he interferes; and he will just hang up without even being asked!".

Ma'am Joanna EDITH: "Of course! Of course! That's all: Of course!, discretion must! How beautiful! I want "my gentleman" also likes me that way! But beware! Not beating me eh! Nor even by manhandling my girl of ten months; even less: beating my son of ten years, eh!".

FRANCK Gerald: "Surely! Surely! That's all surely!, of course! Of course! That's all: Of course!"

Bruno GRANDA: "It goes without saying!"

Joanna EDITH: "As I have said, it is allowed to speak first; and like that, we take the opportunity to listen to those he says!"

FRANCK Gerald: "Okay! That's all indeed!, agreed!, no problem!"

Bruno GRANDA: "No problem, especially for the fact that not only that there are the other phone lines in "the Office"; to be able to react in case of need; but also that it is not us who pay this very, very; very, very well! That's all: Very, very well!, very, very long phone call! It is not we pay the phone bill!".

EDITH: "It is anyway we eh! But indirectly by our taxes!"

FRANCK: "That's all agreed!, indeed!, absolutely!"

BRUNO: "That's all agreed!, by all means!, it's true. That's: Oll Korrect! But."

EDITH: "But?"

BRUNO: "But since it's almost all – those who receive a salary; if not "good wages," which pays! Then we do not even do that much attention to what we own, we pay for the phone Service, for example!".

EDITH: "Listen! Listen to these fine words of love! [I quote]: ""Tell to her very clear; very clearly! That's all: very clearly explicitly!, and uncompromising that my very serious offense that, suddenly, turns out to be unforgivable, was that" "a Romeo" "that displayed towards" "her Juliet", "which he loved; and he still continues to love her above all"; that is to say, he liked; and he continues to love as "a goddess on earth": "a visceral and dangerous jealousy!"

BRUNO: "Sch – sch! "The expelled" will notice that we are observing him; and: we listen at the same time! So he will be ashamed; and he will hang himself the handset, without even so far, being asked to do so!".

EDITH: "So, we continue to listen to him, very quietly; and this, without making noise!".

And Alberto Rodriguez who suspected nothing, quietly continued his call. He said to his friend Robert MERYC: ""... / ...".""

"Tell to her, very clear; very clear; very clearly! That's all: very clearly explicitly!, that my very serious offense that, suddenly turns out to be unforgivable, was that "a Son of Adam" who had too much too loved "his Daughter of Eva"; which, alas!, unfortunately, wrong!"

"Tell to her, very clearly; very clear; very clearly! That's all: very clearly explicitly!, and this without any complacency, that my very serious offense; which, as a result, turns out to be unforgivable, was to love a beautiful girl and that she, "a horse" that displayed towards his "mare", which he loved; and continues to love her above all; that is to say, he liked; and he continues to love as: "a goddess on this Universe", the visceral jealousy; the exacerbated jealousy; and therefore "the dangerous jealousy"."

"But tell to her, I did not know."

"Tell to her, that it was only because I loved her; and I still continue to love her greatly."

"Put to her, very explicitly; very explicitly! That's all: Very explicitly!, the question whether: "What, was it, wrong exactly, exactly! That's all exactly!, to be jealous; or very jealous; in order to try to keep her to himself; and when I say for himself; it's really for yourself; that is to say, for me Alberto Rodriguez myself, the one I really love?"

"Tell to her, very clearly; very clear; very clearly! That's all: very clearly explicitly!, that I could about it, make a billion of letters, or even more; if it would be possible; on which I could have quietly write (1) { : *"If and only if; that is to say: "A billion letters, or even more!". Were lovely and very feasible to be able to write!". Would add Alberto, to Robert.* }, for example: "Irene

LUCINDAÇIO, I love you too! Irene LUCINDAÇIO, I love you too much, too! Irene LUCINDAÇIO, I love you too much, too much, too!"

"ROBERT! Especially confirms to her, very explicitly; explicitly! That's all: Very explicitly!, that now: to have loved too much "hen"; I became as "a hen wet in ice water for example! Hum mm! In wet ice, for example"! Hum mm water! For not to say: "in freezing water!"

"Set to her, very explicitly; very explicitly; explicitly! That's all: Very explicitly!, ROBERT, now that I've got it very well; very well! That's all: Very well!, that we should absolutely; absolutely! That's all absolutely!, not love "a female" (2) { : "Any one: who cares? ", Alberto would clarify it, to Robert. } in that way, as I ALBERTO, I had loved her; and I continue to love her just! Since this is now the race results:"

"A very, very; absolutely! That's all absolutely!, deep split between us; with the added bonus: is the prison for me! Prison for her! And not forget to mention, the process of eviction, committed against me!"

"My friend ROBERT! Tell to IRENE very explicitly, very explicitly! That's all: Very explicitly!, that: I "let" for her, the girl we had together!"

"Remember to her for example, that I had given to her "a brand new BMW car!"

"Remind to her for example that I had also purchased a very, that's all indeed!, agreed!, nice and very, that's all agreed!, indeed!, large pavilion at her country, in Madeira Island, located in the Atlantic Ocean; and which obviously; obviously! That's all: Obviously!, pavilion has indeed, surely! That's all surely!, at her name!"

"Remind to her for example that I had given to her a lot of jewellery and many other things of luxury!"

"Remind to her that I was doing all in its favour, it was with "silk" that I turned in the London account of my father; which father had trusted me yet; and I on my part, I made him show a considerable breach of trust! And that for that? And this for a "Siren" Miss Irene LUCINDAÇIO, she!"

"Remind to her that because of this, me Alberto RODRIGUEZ, I entered say, "out of favour" in the eyes of my father!"

"And all those, that's why?"

"And all of those, it's because I loved; and I love again and again until now always "a mermaid named Irene"!

"Um mm! I demonstrated a significant breach of trust with my dad! And this, for that? And this for a "Siren" Miss Irene LUCINDAÇIO, her!"

And one on of the best. And just happens to Aminata Ayichatoune of "Mali" is exactly; exactly! That's all exactly!, the same.

"Hum mm! For "a Chicken"! Make a considerable breach of trust! And that, for a "Doll"! And who is "this Chick"?"

"And "this Rave" this is her: Miss Irene LUCINDAÇIO!"

"Is this not the irrefutable and the conclusive evidence "of a son of Adam" who too loved "the daughter of Eva"; and that continues, despite himself, to always love her (3) { *: Would say Alberto Rodriguez, at Robert MERYC. *}? For not to say: Is this not the irrefutable and conclusive evidence of "a nobody" in immaturity?"

"And when (4) { *: "That is to say: I RODRIGUEZ!", he would say.* }, which has (5) { *: "This is to say her, IRENE!", he would say later.* } "only was at first that simply enamoured"; and thereafter finally; and that, oddly enough, she had finally, "tied" as "glue" for example! And consequently, she had finished with love too! And that "this gentleman" in question; that is to say, myself Alberto Rodriguez, trunk her suddenly, with "another Bimbo"!"

"A question arises doubt in this case: Does not she have the right to be angry; while losing such downright her head; and therefore act as I had done?"

"Or expressing myself differently. And do all the nonsense's, like all those myself RODRIGUEZ, I committed?"

"That is to say, for example hide downright "staggering" I paid in people I know; up Machiavellian "a conspiracy" with two of my true friends! And say it was beautiful and well she (6) { *: This is to say her, Miss Irene LUCINDAÇIO.* } "the dealer"! And therefore, who sold this cocaine?"

"All of them, it was the consequence of the fact that I loved to "blind love"! My dear friend Robert explain it to her, very explicitly. Very explicitly! That's all: Very explicitly!"

"Tell to her very clearly; very clear; very clearly! That's all: very clearly explicitly!, that I recognize myself very solemnly: it is true that this is quite frankly, no excuse for acting for her, as I had done: for example burn hers clothes and Acts of Civil Status of our child; bully: and "the poor innocent kids"; and even "their mom" to the point of sending her to the hospital, in the Emergency Service!"

"Explain to her, Robert, that I was not myself! I found myself anymore in my normal state!"

"Explain to her, clearly; very clear; very clearly! That's all: very clearly explicitly!, that I had done so; it's because I loved her; and I still love her also still too many; too much, too; too, too, too; sadly and unfortunately, I already felt, leave her inexorably!; and she would go to a certain, certainly! That's all: Certainly!, Lopez Ramiro!"

"Tell her clearly; very clear; very clearly! That's all: very clearly explicitly!, that, which done alas!, unfortunately! Hence, for the events which were quite logically follow, I felt myself already, be imprisoned!"

"Explain to her, very clearly, very clear; very clearly! That's all: very clearly explicitly!, that the new data of the situation, now becoming so! Hence, in order to also deprive LOPEZ, of her

I loved; and I still like always love, I had thought of a double alternative!"

"And what were these two alternatives?"

"It is primarily "the outright trashing"! Then "trashing me as myself later!"

"As, Lopez Ramiro also did nothing! ... / ...! " " "... / ...""""

Bruno GRANDA, one of the Officers of the judicial Police who was listening to Alberto Rodriguez, and speaking to one of his colleagues; that is to say: Gerald FRANCK, he would say: "It! It is serious that, those called "the expelled!".

Gerald FRANCK: ""The expelled" is not an idiot! If he says so himself now! This is because he had already confessed to the judge; and therefore, he had already convicted among others: that crime!".

Bruno GRANDA: "Yeah! Exactly! That's all exactly!, it's true!"

Alberto Rodriguez, continuing to talk to his friend Robert MERYC:"

""And second: or else the dirty (7) { : *Messing Miss Irene LUCINDAÇIO, by accusing her unjustly.* }; the first dirty "as it really should"; "soiling" leading to her therefore, unquestionably, a farm prison!"

""And like that, Lopez Ramiro will hate her; he will drop her; and that, finally!""

"So he would have preferred to find "another old bag"!"

"And let "a little more or less open door" for later, between me and …/… (8) { *: She: IRENE.* }!"

""To resume as before, when a departure; and forget the past!""

""My dear ROBERT! Tell to her, very clearly; very clear; very clearly! That's all: very clearly explicitly!, that it was the anger that had driven me to behave like that!""

"And asked me, "If she was" the foal! "That is to say: "He [Alberto RODRIGUEZ]! And me [she "the filly"]! That is to say: she (9) { *: That is to say: Irene LUCINDAÇIO* }, with all these adventures! She would have done anything to be able to still keep "that" "she loved?"."

""Tell to her, very clearly, very clearly; very clear; very clearly! That's all: very clearly explicitly!, that she meets me quite frankly!""

""That's all right: AYE – AYE!"" Tell to her, very explicitly, very explicitly! That's all: Very explicitly!, as she can remember all those I-listed high (10) { *: "And yet, I have not listed all! This is because those do not matter! Because after all! She had indeed; that's all indeed!, agreed!, been, if only a very small time only: "my favourite goddess", this Universe no! Or at least what I thought!", would say RODRIGUEZ, to ROBERT.* }!""

""That's all right: AYE!"" Tell to her, very explicitly, very explicitly! That's all: Very explicitly!, that I RODRIGUEZ I am "in great disagreement with my parent", because of all those!"

"That's all right: Indeed!, agreed!"" Tell to her, very clearly, very clear; very clearly! That's all: Very clearly explicitly!, that for all these doings there, that me RODRIGUEZ, I was doing for her!"

"That's all right: Agreed!, Indeed!"" What I ask only "two small Papers"; or even "to the limit, only one of these sanctimonious"! The key is that the name RODRIGUEZ, figured on it will be found anyway!"

"That's all right yes!;"" and yes; that's all right: Agreed!, indeed!"" Tell to her, I know very well, very, very well! That's all: Very, very well!, that with "my crazy love" the other day; that is to say, of that fateful day, when everything was ruined forever because of that phone call from Lopez Ramiro!"

"That's all right: YEP!"" That I myself; burned the originals, which ones, I should have kept; while she, with all her efforts, she prevented me; but as I had been, and I admit: fearless and ruthless against her; and that on the contrary, I should beat up her, more for daring to try to make me keep from burning these sanctimonious! It was "a real stupidity" from me!"

"Surely! That's all surely!"" It was really "a real unintelligently" from me!"

"That's: Oll Korrect!"" If only I had scarcely committed "this gaping then" right now, the problem would not even asked! Finally, we often think about it, when it's too much, too late! She had taken me think well before you can burn those Papers! I said: This is too much, too late! But in reality, she could still do something for me! She could even help me! If and only if, however, she agreed; that's all agreed!, indeed!, to do it of course! Of course! That's all: Of course! In doing so!"

"That's all correct!"" In doing so, tell to her, if she holds quite frankly, to help me despite all my nonsense's I've made! ""

"That's all right: OK!"" It has everything and for everything: even twenty four hours to do it! Otherwise it would be too late!""

"That's all right: OKAY!"" She still has twenty four hours to go ask for Duplicates at the City Hall! And send them to me at the Police Station as soon as possible; about it, here is the address of the Office where I find myself: this is (11) { : *"The number 6386 Broadway London SW 1H 0BD.", would say Alberto Rodriguez, to him.* }; or even failing to send them to me at the Police Station, to send them to me at my Lawyer, which here is the address (1) { : *"The N° 527, New Bond Street London W 1Y 9 DD.", would add RODRIGUEZ.* } and the phone number (2). { : *"The N° 00 11 22 33", he would say to him, again.* }.""

"That's all right:" "Tell to her, very clearly, very clear; very clearly! That's all: Very clearly explicitly!, that no matter how! It is always deporting me! And she'll never, ever, see me again, in this British soil; but at least it would leave me a reasonable time, just for the time that my friends and some people in my extended family; whom are here in London can meet me first!""

"That' all right: HUH – HUH!" And they can consequently, make me some purchases; and they can get back "possibly" some gifts; and especially they can go get my clothes in the apartment where she IRENE, now lives; this is because if I tell to her, to bring them for me! I know very well, very, very well! That's all: Very, very well!, she would not accept!"

"That's all right yes!"" Tell to her, that I absolutely; absolutely! That's all absolutely!, need these clothes for me to return at least "clean" in São Paulo;

especially since I finally, spent here in Europe, "quietly" a "decade" without, consider one small moment to return at least once at home in São Paulo exactly! Exactly! That's all exactly!"

"That's all right yes!"" Tell to her, if she does not send me the Civil State Papers, which ones, I asked her; I would hang; and that, without any other form of "trial" over the plane of "Society British Air – Way"; in which space is reserved for me in twenty four hours; and so, I would be expelled all dirty; as I am now, without even a small bag on my hand with me!"

"That's all right yes!;"" and yes!"" And that would be very, verily! That's all verily!, sad for me and my mother."

""That's all right yeah!;"" and yeah!"" Tell to her, that it would be doubly sad; that is to say, for myself, first; and on the other hand: my mother in São Paulo; this is because I just hear the news now that my father, as part of its multiple affairs, he had crashed with a small private jet; and that there were no survivors! And that this had happened there three months already! A plane crash! What a sad end for my father! What tragic death! How sad news for me!""

""In this small private jet, counting the three crew members, there were a total of fourteen people, but there was, as I just said, no survivors!""

""This accident had taken place, there are three months; but since it is not particularly wanted to demoralize me more, with all my worries, due to remaining in everything twice in a prison world! So we had initially preferred that my situation can first be unlocked slightly; so that finally, decides, power anyway, anyway, to tell me this sad news! That is why, we just told me just now only!""

"Tell to her, very clearly, very clearly; very clearly! That's all: Very clearly, explicitly!: if she does not make me send that Civil Status Documents; at least she knows that my Lawyer ["Mistress"] Alcina BARBARA, had done, in spite of herself; and the British justice had indeed, that's all indeed!, agreed!, understood the predicament, which I eventually found; and wanted consequently; *and consequently! That's all: And consequently!*, be indulgent to me; and perhaps also: let me go!"

"But it is indeed; that's all agreed!, indeed!, her, "my Archduchess", for not to saying "my ex – Duchess"; that is to say, her (3) { *: Irene LUCINDAÇIO.* }, who "signed" so to speak, for "her stubborn attitude of negation": "the act of non – indulgence", vis-à-vis me; and even extra: who "signed" "my act of expulsion"."

"Tell to her, very explicitly, very explicitly! That's all: Very explicitly!, that in this case, I certainly; certainly! That's all: Certainly!, would go "pass away" in São Paulo, as a result of various concerns! But in her life, her conscience would now never, ever, never, ever; and never, ever, never, ever, been quiet!"

"And therefore she would always still getting over her; and that, for all the time: "AN OTHER FORM OF TORTURE OF HER OWN CONSCIENCE "!"

""Tell to her very clear; very clearly! That's all: Very clearly, explicitly!, that I had crossed the line; it is because I had loved her; and besides about it, I still love her again and again forever; and I wanted to keep her for myself and not to share her with some Lopez Ramiro!". " ... / ... ". "

Joanna EDITH, addressing to hers colleagues: "Listen my dear colleagues behind this sentence [I quote]: "... / ... This is because I had loved and elsewhere about it, I 'yet again and again like always; and I wanted to keep her for myself and not to sharing her with, some Lopez AMIGO ... / ...!"."."

Gerald FRANCK: ""Ramiro" and not "AMIGO"!".

Joanna EDITH: "" By all means!, that's all correct!, "some Lopez Ramiro!". [End of quote]. What a lovely style!".".

Bruno GRANDA: "How beautiful!".

Gerald FRANCK: "Good! Colleagues, we stop now. We'll stop there; this is because during the whole time, we follow more or less; and therefore, we contemplate his emotions, "the expelled" as to him, he takes advantage of very, very; of very, very well! That's all: Very, very well!, significant telephone Service; and apparently he is not even ready yet, to be able to stop! So.".

Joanna EDITH: "So?"

Gerald FRANCK: "So we'll just break the line for him!".

Joanna EDITH: "Whether it's a shame!".

Bruno GRANDA: "It is frankly admits that "a show – audio" were followed there, so to speak; and even "audio – visual, high – level"; and this, for free; and that's a shame to stop!".

Gerald FRANCK: "It is not at all free! Far from it! It will cost our to Service, too expensive for the phone bill!"

Bruno GRANDA: "Yep!, it's true. That's: Oll Korrect!"

Gerald FRANCK: "Then we'll stop. We will interrupt him, especially since we have a job "the guys"! (colleagues!, did he mean)."

And the Officer Gerald FRANCK would sign himself "the expelled"; that is to say: Alberto Rodriguez to talk to him. That said, the latter, noting that they wanted to talk to him, he said to Robert MERYC, his interlocutor who was on the other end of the line: "A moment! Do not leave ROBERT! We want to talk to me!"

Indeed, that's all indeed!, agreed!, the Officer Gerald FRANCK, listening only the last sentence of RODRIGUEZ and after announcing to his colleagues, that: "We would stop one; it seems therefore that one "and" Sir "deportee"? It's been an eternity that we have been kind enough to release you voluntarily this telephone line one! Enough is enough the very, very long speech! We give you now, only a few seconds, to conclude; this is because, although it is the State that pays the bills; and that we are not employees, who pay directly (4) { *: "Except indirectly through our taxes, of course! Of course! That's all: Of course! "* }; but the telephone lines also two other, began to be saturated! Hence, it really is high time for you now; you can free us from this line you blocked for now, a Century already! There is nice; it is because we are aware of your problem, but anyway! We should not either, abuse! You should be recognized that there are limits to everything!"

That said, Alberto Rodriguez continue to be directed to Robert MERYC, his interlocutor, to conclude. For this, he would say:""Quit" "this long telephone narrative"; not to say, "this long telephone conversation"; and thank greatly "the peace – guardians" who kindly let me quietly call!"

"I Quit "this telephone narration"; and I expect you to me phones to that number for a moment ... / ...!"" ... / ... "."

RODRIGUEZ then would send in one of the Police Officers; saying:""Sir" the Officer! Please! Could you tell me the phone number of here? This is because we are going to call me to give me the result of all those I have just spoken to a friend of mine; which will come into contact with "my ex – regular"!".

And "Sir" the Officer Gerald FRANCK, who had addressed RODRIGUEZ, would reply: "It's the number: 12 34 56 78."

RODRIGUEZ, to the Officer FRANCK: "Ah! I do not even have me here, a pen and paper to write it down!"

The Officer FRANCK: "But! But there is no risk to forget such a number; because just count only: 1, to 8; then there you go! But, anyway take this pen and piece of paper here, for the record!", would specify the Officer FRANCK, to the "expelled" RODRIGUEZ.

RODRIGUEZ: "Thank you, "Sir" the Officer!".

The Officer FRANCK: "Ready?"

RODRIGUEZ: "Aye! That's all aye!, ready!"

The Officer FRANCK: "So, this is the N° 12 – 34 – 56 – 78."

RODRIGUEZ: "Thank you "Sir" (5) {: *And then Alberto RODRIGUEZ continues to turn to his friend Robert MERYC to transmit this phone number, which one he had received on the part of the Officer Gerald FRANCK.* }!".

And then RODRIGUEZ would say to R. MERYC: "ROBERT?"

ROBERT: "Aye – aye! That's all aye – aye!, ih!, ih, ih!"

A. RODRIGUEZ: "Note this number. This is the N° 12 – 34 – 56 – 78. And there is not a risk to forget such a number; simply because in that case, count only 1 to 8; and further notes the phone number of Mistress Alcina BARBARA, my Lawyer; and even her address; cause, IRÈNE could, in that case; if and only if she would like it: direct contact Mistress Alcina BARBARA!"

ROBERT: "Give them!"

RODRIGUEZ: "She lives at N° 527 New Bond Street London W 1Y 9 SD; and her telephone number is 00 – 11 – 22 – 33. And once again, there is no risk to forget such a number; because just count only: 0 to 3; but by repeating each time, these four figures in question."

ROBERT: "Uh – huh! That's all uh – huh!, it's highly rated!"

And it was that way, that Alberto Rodriguez concluded his "very, very long telephone – narration" tolerated by the Police Guards. He was about to say: "Goodbye!" Robert MERYC."

Then, just this one would say to RODRIGUEZ: "RODRIGUEZ! Wait a minute or two! The both phone numbers and the two addresses that you have dictated to me, I noted only by heart; then I go to this account, that it is unwise for me! Because, although apparently these two numbers seem easy to remember! But you never, ever know! I may nevertheless; *nevertheless! That's all: Nevertheless!*, to forget them anyway; and this, even before that I can enter in contact with IRENE! That said, wait just a second, I go and get a paper and a pen, so you me once more rehearsals!".

RODRIGUEZ: "Okay That's all Okay!, I expect (6). { : *Then a few seconds later, Robert MERYC returned on the other side of the line; and he said: –––. }.".*

ROBERT: "I am ready now."

RODRIGUEZ: "Then the telephone number of the Police Station where I am now, is: 1 – 2 – 3 – 4 – 5 – 6 – 7 – 8. (7). { : *And then Alberto RODRIGUEZ repeat it: the telephone number of his Lawyer; the address of the Police Station where he was again (after once having yet again, asked himself, with one of the Officers on duty, for confirmation); and finally, the address of his Lawyer. ". }.*

ROBERT: "This time, all is well noted."

RODRIGUEZ: "When you gonna call for me!"

ROBERT: "Yes ih! That's all right yes!, ih, ih!"

RODRIGUEZ: "You say that you want to speak with "Alberto RODRIGUEZ, the expelled"! Indeed. That's all indeed!, agreed!".

ROBERT: "Indeed? That's all indeed!, agreed?"

RODRIGUEZ: "Besides, I am only the "only deportable" and "the only expelled" for the moment, in all the Police here! So there is no risk of being wrong!"

ROBERT: "That said?"

RODRIGUEZ: "That said, I will hang up; and I look forward to your call!"

ROBERT: "No problem RODRIGUEZ!"

If him Alberto Rodriguez, he finally, felt then for example, have in him some weight in his consciousness about the evil, which one he had done "at the back then", to Madam Valery GLED, wife REDLER!

Was it then already: time to call: and it precisely; and "old" boss Imbourt GUERIN; and "old" friend Haman GENSEN; and several different people; which serve therefore like the witnesses; so finally: to "beat" publicly and solemnly, "his coulpa" ("to repent one's sins openly") [in order to beat his breast]; and maybe this way, the spirits hidden; which severely chastised in this way, would eventually have mercy on him; and consequently; *and consequently! That's all: And consequently!*, they would eventually make too; and this: rather Mysteriously; *mysteriously! That's all: Mysteriously!*, so as to relieve from all the harassment that they knew; which in reality were directly, related and Irrationally, the harm that himself Alberto Rodriguez had unfairly done to Madam Valery GLED, wife REDLER?

"... / ... Why talk about this manure there? Why talk about this sick one? Why talks about this plague that? ... / ....".

And Alberto Rodriguez had finally, hung up the telephone handset wall. Immediately after, Robert MERYC; which saw little: Where to start talking, all long message, addressed to Miss Irene LUCINDAÇIO; he nevertheless; *nevertheless! That's all: Nevertheless!*, preferred to be very succinct. That said, he had taken his telephone device; he had called her. He did not even know that she had for example, found work as a "maid"; and that, for the morning and evening hours only; and for that very reason, she was never, ever to return home before 21 hours 00' – 21 30' times.

Despite this, Robert MERYC, given the urgency of the message to be transmitted; he insisted; and after the tenth attempt, he finally, got a person on the phone.

It was not João – Santos BARRAY 's cousin IRENE L.; which ultimately always lived with her; but it was the voice of "a Princess".

And that was her, "this Arian?"

It was herself Miss Irene LUCINDAÇIO, the "Agnes" or rather "the former Artemis" of Alberto RODRIGUEZ.

In doing so, ROBERT says to that one: "Hello IRENE! This is the part of me ROBERT! Robert MERYC! ".

IRENE: "Ah! ROBERT Hello!"

Robert MERYC: "Hello IRENE! "

IRENE: "Ah!, ROBERT! This is a lease huh!"

ROBERT: "Agreed! That's all agreed!, indeed!, it's true."

IRENE: "It's been a long time since we lived with RODRIGUEZ, you phoned us! But since all the events that I had with him, do we ... / ...!"

ROBERT: "I will phone you again!"

IRENE: "Okay! That's: Oll Korrect!, indeed! That's all indeed!, agreed! You do phone us again! So."

ROBERT: "So?"

IRENE: "So "what good or evil wind" that pushes you to do that today? "What good or bad wind" pushes you to call me at that hour or so late? Since it is already 9:18 p.m. specified (1) { : *"To my pendulum ", would say IRENE, to ROBERT.* }; while I'm barely back from my work; and I'm totally tired?"

ROBERT: "Excuse me for this, but given the urgency!"

IRENE: ""But given the urgency?"

ROBERT: "Certainly. Certainly! That's all: Certainly! Given the urgency of the problem! For this, I'll call you!"

IRENE: "What is this pressing problem?"

ROBERT: "It's been a total of nine times already since the beginning of that evening, I started to call you!"

IRENE: "It's normal that you could hardly get me on the phone! That's because I was still at that time, in my work as "cleaning woman"; and then on the way back, to return home here!"

ROBERT: "I did not know you were working until later in the evening!"

IRENE: "Unfortunately, alas!, righty – ho! That's all agreed!, indeed!, I work until later. But as I work my day in two times (2) { : *Morning and evening.* }!

So in the day; or rather, in the time period from the middle of the day, I am on my door in the remains huh!"

Robert MERYC: "Finally! I did not know! This is what was such that every time I called!"

Irene LUCINDAÇIO " Uh – huh!, ih!, ih! That's: Oll Korrect! Continue; I'm listening! That's what made sure, surely! That's all surely!, that every time you phoned?"

ROBERT: "That's what was so, that every time I called! I came across one at all! And even on your cousin João – SANTOS, so I left him a message!"

IRENE: "Oh!, my cousin!"

ROBERT: "Of course! That's all: Of course!, ih!, ih, ih!"

IRENE: "When he heard that I was only probably get my kids to the Services for "EWO / ESW"; the "LEA" and "CA" while maintaining my job; otherwise ... / ...."

Robert MERYC: "Exactly! That's all exactly!, ih!, ih, ih!"

Irene LUCINDAÇIO: "Otherwise I would have had such serious difficulties; even very serious difficulties; see: very, very serious difficulties to meet all the daily needs that affect us and not forgetting those on maintenance, care and cetera and so on ... of the apartment; if ever by chance, I had to abandon my work! "

Robert MERYC: "Obviously! That's all Obviously!, ih!, ih, ih!"

IRENE: "Otherwise I would have had such a very, very serious difficulties to meet all the daily needs of myself and my children."

ROBERT: "Surely! That's all surely!, ih!, ih, ih!"

IRENE: "For this, I told my cousin João – Santos BARRAY: I would definitely need his help in order to accompany the children, especially the youngest, morning and evening, at the "Day Nursery" [Nursery] or the Nurse 3 { *: "It would depend, of course, of course! That's all: Of course!, what I would have us opportunity!", she would say to him.* }; and if you count my eldest child, to bring him, to him as to the "Primary School" [at Primary School], at least some winter days only, where it is very, very dark! And that."

ROBERT: "What?"

IRENE: "And as for his work of Guardian of Supermarket, his schedules are for him, very well; very, very well! That's all: Very, very well!, "facts"! Since he does not begin until 10 hours 00'; up to 18 hours 00'! And in addition, the Supermarket in question is only a couple hundred meters from where we live! From where ... / ...."

ROBERT: "And what did he say?"

IRENE: "Wait! Hence, he would have ample time to accompany the kids to 08 H 30′, and retrieved 18 H 30. And you know what he told me, listening to this?".

ROBERT: "No!"

IRENE: "Listening to this, my cousin João – Santos BARRAY had always told me [I quote]: "I flatly refused to provide such a task. I refuse especially as it is not me: their father ... / ...!".

ROBERT: "Aye – aye! That's all aye – aye!, ih!, ih, ih! "From"? Continue; I'm listening!"

IRENE: "This is not me, the father of these two kids; and consequently, I absolutely; absolutely! That's all absolutely!, refuse to play "the Dad – chicken "!"

ROBERT: "He told you that? While living at your home! What ingratitude!"

IRENE: "Wait! Although if he had said it! That said, you have not yet heard "the best"! This is because, if it were not for that refusal, I was going to finally, say to him: I don't care!".

ROBERT: "But?"

IRENE: "But he then added [I still quote]: "... / ... Unless that in return, and that's really the case to say finally: that we forget that we have such a percentage significant, of the same blood running through our veins! Forget, both of us, "this side inbreeding" for example; one side much maligned by the moral and hospital orders; or rather, much maligned by the medical orders! You know what I want to tell to you IRENE? You got it my message?". [End of quote].".

And one on of the best. And just happens to Aminata Ayichatoune of "Mali" is exactly; exactly! That's all exactly!, the same.

ROBERT: "Really?"

IRENE: "Yeah! That's all yeah! Yep! That's all yep!, uh – huh!".

ROBERT: "He told you that?"

IRENE: "Bluntly!"

ROBERT: "Had he not seen other ladies out there? Which do not have the same blood as you?"

IRENE: "It ah!"

ROBERT: "Tell me!"

IRENE: "I did not even want to waste "my breath", to tell him about it! I was very, very angry; and it was evident right away by my silence and "closed my face" something I had suddenly adopted! An extreme look crazy!".

ROBERT: "He dared to say to you? Say that, in his own cousin! It ah! What kind of world in which we live!"

IRENE: "Yes ih! That's all right yes!, he bluntly told me that! And this, without even so much as using the smallest detour huh!"

ROBERT: "Ah!, well say so! "Mprrr"! He had "the nerve" to tell you!"

IRENE: "And before the appearance of the farm angry that I had suddenly adopted; and without even as much as I meet him about "his bestial solicitation", my cousin João – Santos BARRAY, himself, then he would let me hear … / …!".

ROBERT: "When he felt very sad seriously your astonishment and desolation!"

IRENE: "Not forget to say: "disarray"; or rather "frustration"! Absolutely yep! Absolutely! That's all absolutely!: Oll Korrect!".

ROBERT: "It's because he certainly; certainly! That's all: Certainly!, scared as you denounce him, near the members of your family!"

IRENE: "That's for sure! Surely! That's all surely! Thing I did, alas!, unfortunately; *unfortunately, alas! That's all: Unfortunately, alas!,* not! And yet I might have had to actually do it!"

ROBERT: "And yeah! That's all yeah! It took immediately denounce!"

IRENE: "Then I said … / … Hence, my cousin was scared himself; and then he let me hear that in addition [I quote]: "… / …! ".

ROBERT: "Yeah! That's: Oll Korrect!, ih!, ih, ih!"

IRENE: ""In addition", "my job to Watch the Store", where I put almost standing for Eight hours straight, "I need to sleep very well every evening, early, to be in form, the next morning!".".

ROBERT: "It was then finally, a mere pretext; it's because you had refused his advances!"

IRENE: "Absolutely! Absolutely! That's all absolutely! And I asked him what he meant by "sleep very well every evening, early"?".

ROBERT: "And what did he say?"

IRENE: "He told me [I quote]: ""Sleep very well every evening, early"; that is to say: do not wake up for example at Eight in the morning.".".

ROBERT: "Now with this task you wanted to trust him! There was talk that he wakes up every day early!"

IRENE: "Now with this task I wanted to assign to him; it was question indeed: That's all indeed!, agreed!, he wakes downright 4 { : "In later!", she would clarify it. } for every day of work, at 07 H 10 'In the morning! But hundreds of thousands of people wake up in this country at this time eh; even earlier than that ah!".

ROBERT: "By the way: if I look fine, only about an hour's sacrifice anything!".

IRENE: "Exactly! That's all exactly! Only about an hour's sacrifice; and that, just Five days a week; not Seven days a week!"

ROBERT: "But?".

IRENE: "But my cousin João – Santos BARRAY was even preferred to go out himself, from "my home"; without that I IRENE, I ask him to do that! He had gone by himself, listening only what I tried to ask him to do for the benefit of my children.".

ROBERT: "Hence, the project can recover your "kids" with the "EWO / ESW"; the "LEA" and "CA", could therefore: being delayed; especially for not saying by example: "What this project can recover your kids could consequently; *and consequently! That's all: And consequently*: being postponed indefinitely!".".

Irene LUCINDAÇIO: "Absolutely! Absolutely! That's all absolutely! Hence my project about to recover as soon as possible, my son Ernesto DOMINGUEZ and my girl Elisio GOMEZ RODRIGUEZ, from the "EWO / ESW"; the "LEA" and "CA" could consequently; *and consequently! That's all: And consequently*: being delayed by myself of course; of course! That's all: Of course!, and that for a long time; this is because.".

Robert MERYC: "This is because?"

IRENE: "It's because I do not know yet, when is it that I could be "quiet and without trouble" with my current job; and then forward somehow, to accompany "my kids" at school and Nursery, mornings and evenings, Five days a week! Unless!".

Robert MERYC: "Unless?"

IRENE: "Unless I have a chance; if this could result "very soon", as I had promised one of the Social Workers, who are actively working for me, in that sense; "Change of job," and consequently, to find for me, where the schedules would be something close, as being those of "my cousin João – Santos BARRAY " for example!".

ROBERT: "It's a possibility yeah!, ih!"

IRENE: "Going back to what you were saying, that for nine attempts from the early evening today, that you just could not join me; or even join my cousin João – Santos BARRAY, to leave "the urgent message"! I ... / ...!".

ROBERT: "Obviously! That's all Obviously!, ih!, ih, ih!"

IRENE: "I will summarize briefly, that João – Santos BARRAY is left home; and it's been a while! He left without even as much as I IRENE, I ask him to do that! Tarnish for what he had dared to ask forced – what!"

ROBERT: "Affirmative! That's all affirmative! I quite understand."

IRENE: "So after your tenth attempt, you've had myself!"

ROBERT: "Of course! That's all: Of course!, and that, at 21 H 18 precise 's, exactly! Exactly! That's all exactly!"

IRENE: "It's like I told to you: it's for the simple reason that from Monday to Friday, I go home at this hour, almost!"

ROBERT: "Okay. That's all agreed!, indeed! Like what, I was right to insist!"

IRENE: "But against, from 11 H 15; up to 15 H 45', I'm at home in the apartment. I might occasionally take time off to go do a few shopping by example; but usually not for very long time! Nevertheless!"

ROBERT: "Aye – aye! That's all indeed!, agreed! Nevertheless?"

IRENE: "However, I've never, ever heard you call me, since "a long, a long time" already!".

ROBERT: "Excuse me then! But for today, I telephoned you anyway! I started around 18 H 49; and I repeated, while "ten times" from that hour! Hence almost!".

IRENE: "Where about?"

ROBERT: "Where roughly once, on average, every fifteen minutes; and until at the end of the tenth time I heard you finally, had a phone call away!"

IRENE: "So! You want to tell me what to do?"

ROBERT: "I wanted to actually talk to you, about your ex – RODRIGUEZ!"

IRENE: "From RODRIGUEZ!

But!

""–That's all right: AYE – AYE!" "But why talk to me about this manure there?

""–That's all right: AYE!" ""Why talk to me about this sick one?

""–That's all right: Indeed!, agreed!" ""Why talk to me about this plague that?

""–That's all right: Agreed!, Indeed!!" ""Why talk to me about this demon that?

""–That's all right yes!;" "and yes; that's all right: Agreed!, indeed!" ""Why talk to me about him?

""–That's all right: YEP!"" Huh?

""Surely! That's all surely!"" –ROBERT answer me!

""That's: Oll Korrect!" ""–But answer me ROBERT!

""That's all correct!" ""–But you've fallen by the head or what?

""That's all right: OK!" ""–But stop your whining ROBERT!

""That's all right: OKAY!" ""–But Robert, you've lost a little ball or what?

""That's all right: ""–Me IRENE, I have given so much of myself, at RODRIGUEZ!

""That' all right: HUH – HUH!" ""–So eh!

""That's all right yes!" ""–Enough now!

""That's all right yeah!, and yes!" ""–When I think for example: How I loved him; upon himself the moment that we had met in a tavern!

""That's all right yes!;"" and yes!" ""–When I think for example: That I was already very ready "to lie down with him"; upon himself the moment that we had met in the tavern in question!

""That's all right yeah!;"" and yeah!!" ""–And he RODRIGUEZ, as to him, he made me those he did to me!

""That's all right: AYE – AYE!" ""–So it ah!, he really spit in the soup what!

""That's all right: AYE!" ""–Now, to live in harmony with others requires not particularly little spit in the soup!

""That's all right: Indeed!, agreed!" ""–And apparently; apparently! That's all: Apparently!, it seems that Rodriguez did not even know it!

""That's all right: Agreed!, Indeed!!" ""–And you ROBERT you plead for him with me!

""That's all right yes!;" "and yes; that's all right: Agreed!, indeed!" ""–So it ah, this is the bouquet!

""That's all right: YEP!" ""–It really is the bouquet!

""Surely! That's all surely!" ""–Why ROBERT, you worry you make the case?

""That's: Oll Korrect!" ""–Why are you mounted pin?

""That's all correct!" ""–Alberto RODRIGUEZ, this is a real mentee!

""That's all right: OK!" ""So eh!

""That's all right: OKAY!" ""It's a real religious mentee!

""That's all right:" ""So eh!

""That' all right: HUH – HUH!" ""He was trashing me!

""That's all right yes!" ""Besides, I was out as a result of a miracle that we could not even at all, at all, to explain!

""That's all right yeahl, and yesl" ""He even abused children (that is to say, the baby including [And especially for the elder to him as he had systematically beaten, as he had beaten me, IRENE!].).

""That's all right yes!;" "and yes!" ""It was really strange huh!, for having done this!

""That's all right yeah!;"" and yeah!!" ""It was really strange!

""That's all right: AYE – AYE!" ""Much stranger than a science – fiction – film, for example!

""That's all right: AYE!" ""Do not talk yourself for example, about the binnacle; which one, he had flatly turned upside down! That's all right: YEAH!: Let's not even talk about, for example, the cabin that he had flatly turned upside down!

""That's all right: Indeed!, agreed!" ""ALBERTO is someone who enters a period of time:

""That's all right: Agreed!, Indeed!!," ""the good climate of understanding "hymen", at a fantastic aggression;

""That's all right yes!;" "and yes; that's all right: Agreed!, indeed!," ""then: from the dreaded aggression, at the euphoria;

""That's all right: YEP!" ""Then: from the euphoria, at the lethargy;

""Surely! That's all surely!," ""and after the course is easily reversed with him; since he is often found, that, he passes from the lethargy, at the euphoria;

""That's: Oll Korrect!," ""from the euphoria, at the dreaded aggressiveness;

""That's all correct!," ""from the dreaded aggressive, at the right climate matrimonial agreement.

""That's all right: OK!" ""This is a problem with him!

""That's all right: OKAY!" ""It's really a big problem with him!

""That's all right:" ""Of course!, of course! That's all: Of course!, in the couple, ALBERTO, it's finally, a "bona fide" problem; an authentic problem!

""That' all right: HUH – HUH!" ""Me IRENE otherwise, I am the solution, so to speak; a real solution!

""That's all right yes!" ""But just now, I'd rather be me; rather than him; I prefer to be the solution; rather, that being the problem!

""That's all right yeah!, and yes!" ""But that's just him ALBERTO with his character of pig; ALBERTO him, with the real problem; he does now, gonna fetching the solution elsewhere; anymore question, at home with me, definitely!

""That's all right yes!;" "and yes!" ""I really wonder: If he, Alberto Rodriguez could he honestly, live a good point, with "a Damsel"; and this, in very good intelligence and truly respect as you respect its "legitimate"!".

Robert MERYC: "You know IRENE!".

Irene LUCINDAÇIO: "No I do not know!"

Robert MERYC: "You know IRENE! Your marital problems! Your love problems appear to be in my opinion, as: some stories, the most unusual love; which may exist!

You know IRENE!

Hum mm!

Your stories of love to you both!

These are truly the stories huh!

Frankly love stories of:

"Ulysses" and "Penelope" (Odysseus and Penelope), for example; or:

"Hector" and "Andromache" (Hector and Andromache) for example; of the poet HOMER (Greek: Homeros); poet whom it is customary to attribute authorship of epic poems of the Eighth Century before Christ: "The Iliad"; "The Odyssey" and "Hymns"; or:

"Mark Antony" and "Cleopatra VII" ([Mark] Antony and Cleopatra), for example, (admittedly, a true story by among – others: Part of Rome and ancient Egypt, but prevents much so far, that it was also: a drama of William Shakespeare [1606]); or:

"Romeo" and "Juliet" (Romeo and Juliet), for example, (drama in Five Acts by William Shakespeare always [1594-1595]); or:

> so many other love stories (known or not known to the public [as an example: the love of Maryvonne KEVILER and Julio Fernandez History]); which love stories in question, it is not even useful to list them all – here; all – these love stories will really turn out to be: that the vulgar lovers of love stories, alongside love story of Alberto Rodriguez and Irene LUCINDAÇIO.

All the characters in these love stories mentioned before, were so to say, the true fans, before such Master and Mistress; which were: of him, Alberto Rodriguez and of you, Irene LUCINDAÇIO; which as to them, they had virtually been: The True Professional Love Stories.

All the characters in These Love Stories mentioned before that of him, Alberto Rodriguez and you, Irene LUCINDAÇIO, as it were: The Real Apprentices 5 . Cfr.: Isaac Mampuya Samba: "A True untimely Awareness".

"Hum mm!

ALBERTO is someone who enters a period of time:

> from the good climate of understanding "hymen", at a fantastic aggression;

> then: from the dreaded aggression, at the euphoria;

then: from the euphoria, at the lethargy;

and after the course is easily reversed with him; since he is often found, that he passes from the lethargy, at the euphoria;

from the euphoria, at the dreaded aggressiveness;

from the dreaded aggressive, at the right climate matrimonial agreement.".

Oh!, oh, oh! Gently! Let us be calm! Why all these qualifiers there? But why all these qualifiers on him? But really: why all these qualifiers, about him?".

IRENE: "Yet that.".

ROBERT: "Again that?".

Irene LUCINDAÇIO: "Yet it is not then, as well moderate qualifiers; when I ... / ...!".

"So there ... / ... I›m really ... / ... very, very; that's all: very, very sorry to let you hear: "That he will wait long! Long! Long, long time, if I counting on me Irene ... / ....""

Irene LUCINDAÇIO would answer "on the reaction"; or rather, about the question; or to put it more precisely; *precisely! That's all: Precisely!*, she would reply "to the astonishments"; or "at the questions": "Oh!, oh, oh! Gently! Let us be calm! But why all these qualifiers on him? Why really all the qualifiers then about him? "Expressed by Robert MERYC, at the attention of Miss Irene LUCINDAÇIO in answering to him; that is to say, in answer to that one precisely: "Yet it is not then, as well the moderate qualifiers; when I think of all the suffering he had inflicted on me himself in person; and of course; of course! That's all: Of course!, if I also I think of all the suffering he had made inflicted indirectly me! ".

ROBERT: "Okay! That's: Oll Korrect!, I understand you!"

IRENE: "Finally, so be it! And you want to tell me what, about him Alberto Rodriguez ?"

ROBERT: "He came out of "jail"!".

IRENE: "He came out of "detention center"?".

ROBERT: "Affirmative! That's all affirmative!"

IRENE: "I thought so well!"

ROBERT: "Why "you suspected you well?".

IRENE: "I knew it well; this is because there are only two days exactly! Exactly! That's all exactly! He phoned me! But!"

ROBERT: "But?"

IRENE: "But as soon as I had only heard his voice on the phone! And since I do not like at all, at all feel as a result of "his Machiavellian and dreadful conspiracy", that he had deliberately mounted against me!".

ROBERT: "Yes ih! That's all right yes!, ih, ih!".

IRENE: "Then, when I had only heard his voice, I'd even not let him the time to present; and I consequently; *and consequently! That's all: And consequently!,* immediately, hang up the handset!"

ROBERT: "And like that you could not even know, for example: From where he called? Or if he is already out of the penitentiary? Or to put it better myself: If it is almost out from the jailhouse, what?"

IRENE: "No! I could not know! I could not know as you say ROBERT: If Rodriguez is already out of "the correctional facility"! Or if he is almost out! Or even if he is still up in prison! Or if he is calling from everywhere! I actually could not know, especially since, in truth!".

ROBERT: "Especially in truth?"

IRENE: "Especially in truth, "I do not care" madly (1) { : *"So to speak", would add she.* } now!".

ROBERT: "Very well!; very, very well! That's all: Very, very well!, I quite understand your bitterness toward him, definitely!".

IRENE: "ROBERT?"

ROBERT: "Aye! That's all aye!, ih!, ih, ih!"

IRENE: "Robert MERYC?"

ROBERT: "Aye – aye! That's all aye – aye!, ih!, ih! I listen! I listen IRENE! Speak so!".

IRENE: "We'll have good, I confess to you that Alberto Rodriguez recalled several times perhaps that "twelve times"! Or maybe less than that!".

ROBERT: "Or maybe more than that?".

IRENE: "It's possible! Or maybe more than that! And I do not even remember! But what I remember!"

ROBERT: "Yeah! That's all yeah!, ih!, ih, ih!"

IRENE: "That every time ... / ...!".

ROBERT: "Yep! That's all yep!, ih!, ih, ih! What every time?".

IRENE: "It has every time when he only wanted to present to me! And that!".

ROBERT: "What?".

IRENE: "And me on my side, whenever I heard his voice only!".

ROBERT: "Yes! That's all OK!, ih, ih, ih!".

IRENE: "So there!"

ROBERT: "So that?"

IRENE: "So it, I immediately hung up the phone on his nose!".

ROBERT: "So you did not let him at all, "a slightest chance" to be able to tell you what!".

IRENE: "Absolutely! Absolutely! That's all absolutely!

After all he had done to me and to the children!

But this turns out to be a logic that I cannot leave for him, now "no slightest chance" no! It is quite logical; because now I ... / ...!....".

ROBERT: "Verily! Absolutely! That's all verily!,

Certainly that this proves to be a logic that you cannot leave for him now "no slightest chance"! But only here, very happily on this planet called "Earth", not everything turns out hardly be necessarily logical.".

IRENE: "It is quite logical; because now I hate him, as if for example, "the plague"; or even worse than the plague; I wanted to say!".

ROBERT: "What do you want: your reaction is well and truly normal huh!, having had to endure, those he had done to you both: directly than indirectly! And I understand you very, very well eh! Very, very well! That's all: Very, very well! He was very bad and very, very mean towards you!

You, who had given to him, so much and yet loves, which ones "an Eva" cans offer to "her Adam"! You, who had yet given to him, so a pretty little girl! He had in return, but to be good vis-à-vis you eh! And like that, everything would have worked best for you both!".

IRENE: "So like that, RODRIGUEZ is downright out of the lock – up? He came out of "jail"?".

ROBERT: "That is to say: "Yes!" And "No!"!".

IRENE: "That is to say: "Yes!" And "No!".".

ROBERT: "Absolutely! Absolutely! That's all absolutely!".

IRENE: "It means?".

ROBERT: "This means that "the plate" as you like to call him (2) { : "As such! ", would clarify at her, ROBERT. } by yourself, is indeed; that's all agreed!, indeed!, beautiful and well done!".

IRENE: "But?".

ROBERT: "But now we want to ship him, to São Paulo, nearby with his family. He who has lost his father, by plane crash (3). { : "There is just three months", would say ROBERT, at IRENE. Including the three crew members, plus eleven businessmen who were in the small private jet, there were in all: fourteen ... / ... ". }.

IRENE: "Fourteen people!".

ROBERT: "That's right. And none survivor!".

IRENE: "Wait, ["wait", "wait", "wait"] a moment! He just lost his Dad?".

ROBERT: "Affirmative. Affirmative! That's all affirmative! It happened there exactly; exactly! That's all exactly!, three months ago! But it only took him aware that now! Him, that we would just, coincidentally, return him to his country, as being "an ordinary parcel post" by free; that is to say, ... / ...!".

IRENE: "The businessman called "Eliodoro RODRIGUEZ" is dead there three months already!".

ROBERT: "Absolutely! That's all absolutely! And in this circumstance almost there, one would like to send his son Alberto Rodriguez at his home as "an ordinary parcel post"; that is to say: while "dirty"; one trousers; one shirt; a single pair of shoes; one liner; one pea coat; meaning: he carries articles for a long time now; and already worn out; and other items without more, what!".

IRENE: "Wait, [wait, "wait", "wait", "wait", "wait"] a little time yet eh! Not too fast eh!".

ROBERT: "Verily! That's all verily!, ih!, ih, ih! I wait quietly ih!, aye – aye! That's all aye – aye!".

IRENE: "Wait! You're telling me there, he just lost his dad (4) { : *A businessman.* }? And by airplane accident did you say?".

ROBERT: "Exactly! That's all exactly! It was a small private jet; and there were no survivors of the eleven passengers and the three crew members, after "the crash"!".

IRENE: "It's really sad! And one does not come to him acquaint barely even?".

ROBERT: "Surely! That's all surely!, it was feared that he be more wrong, in announcing this new almost instantly; that is to say, when we did not even have yet, "a slightest idea" how, on the way, going to unlock his case!".

IRENE: "It's sad! Frankly, you can believe my emotion, it's really sad! And then we want to send his son RODRIGUEZ, as "a vulgar parcel", returned to the sender!".

ROBERT: "Verily! That's all verily!".

IRENE: "So there! If the death of his father I am honestly very sad; that's all very, very sad! But nevertheless, being very honest also about the expulsion of his son ALBERTO! I would not say at all, at all; although I should confess: I'm sad! On the contrary, I am very, very happy; that's all I am very, very happy; to hear this news! Since those he had put to me through! In any case, "Everything pays itself down here!", they say! Here even now the irrefutable and undeniable proof!".

ROBERT: "Surely! That's all surely!".

IRENE: "... / ... Send him home in Sao Paulo, "all dirty"?".

ROBERT: "Indeed!, that's all indeed!, agreed!".

IRENE: ""With one pair of trousers?".".

ROBERT: "That's all agreed!, indeed!".

IRENE: ""With a single shirt?".".

ROBERT: "Agreed! That's all agreed!, indeed!".

IRENE: ""With a single pea coat?".".

ROBERT: "That's it, yes! That's all right yes!".

IRENE: ""With a single pair of shoes?".".

ROBERT: "By all means! That's: Oll Korrect!".

IRENE: ""All of the old articles, he wore; and he always wears, very long time"?".

ROBERT: "All right! That's all right!"

IRENE: "That is to say, almost all worn; or very worn; for not to say, "damaged or torn?".".

ROBERT: "Aye! That's all aye! That's all aye – aye!"

IRENE: ""And no other articles more"?".

ROBERT: "That's right! That's all right yes!".

IRENE: "In any case! I would have no remorse for him Alberto RODRIGUEZ! I might add that I am glad that it happens like this, for him, after all!".

ROBERT: "His Lawyer, "Mistress" Alcina BARBARA, whose the address is as follows: If, however, you wish to note it?".

IRENE: "Oh!, there! And for what?"

ROBERT: "Okay! That's all Okay!, you have "nothing to do with this address!".".

IRENE: "Not at all, at all!"

ROBERT: "You accept perhaps, to note the telephone number of that Lawyer? Since I have also, where … / …! "

IRENE: "Oh!, no! No, no! No, no! At all, at all!"

ROBERT: "Not at all, at all, at all?".

IRENE: "Absolutely! Absolutely! That's all absolutely! Not at all, at all, at all! Not at all, at all! That's all not at all, at all, at all!"

ROBERT: "Okay! That's all Okay!, I quite understand!"

IRENE: "I IRENE, I'm doing actually the very, very big efforts to get to completely forget Alberto RODRIGUEZ, from my head! And believe me ROBERT! It is not at all clear! So in such circumstances! Go see him! Hum mm! Go see him! Or even just going to see his Lawyer Mistress Alcina BARBARA! Or just call her! So then, it is impossible to want to ask me that, my dear Robert, with all the respect I owe to you yet!".

ROBERT: "Yeah! That's all yeah!, I understand your feeling of "disgust"; which you now against him Alberto RODRIGUEZ. Well, I meant just that, his Lawyer had provided a significant effort not to do that more expels Alberto Rodriguez (5) { : *"No, no! Not at all for that! There was no question that his Lawyer, do it!*

Because, no matter how, him Alberto RODRIGUEZ would be anyway expelled!", would clarify him Robert MERYC, at her interlocutor Irene LUCINDAÇIO. }! But."

IRENE: "But?"

ROBERT: "But we give him only a reasonable time, just long enough so that all his living by example, "this" Metropolis of London", come meet him in the Office where he is currently found! And above.".

IRENE: "And above all?"

ROBERT: "And above all, for one of his example, may first have time to spend with you; that is to say: "on the third floor of N° 122 Tottenham Court Road, London W1" ... / ....".

IRENE: "And do what?"

ROBERT: "To collect and recover almost all the most common Personal Effects; including his clothes; since, according to him ... / .... ".

IRENE: "Uh – huh! That's: Oll: Uh – huh!, ih! Since according to him?"

ROBERT: "Since according to him, if he asks you to go collect; and bring them to him; you certainly; certainly! That's all: Certainly!, would not agree to do that!"

IRENE: "For it ah! He had not come slip up! He had hardly deceived; for the simple reason that, I Irene LUCINDAÇIO, I do not do anything at all, at all, that would help so slightly RODRIGUEZ! On the contrary, if I can do all, I could do, in order: to be able to put him (or rather: he put a lot more, if and only if the opportunity or opportunities "presented themselves to me)" "sticks on wheels", I would not hesitate especially hardly at all, at all, only a little while, I, Irene LUCINDAÇIO, to do that; to push that even further!".

And one on of the best. And just happens to Aminata Ayichatoune of "Mali" is exactly; exactly! That's all exactly!, the same.

ROBERT: "Yeah! That's all yeah!, I understand you very well! Very, very well! That's all: Very, very well! This is why his Lawyer would get for him "more time" so that we can prepare to him just anyway, his clothes and luggage for someone … / ….".

IRENE: "Yep! That's all yep!, ih!, ih, ih! For someone?"

ROBERT: "For someone who has spent a decade finally 6 { : [So to speak!]. }, in Europe, without being able to return at home in Sao Paulo; can anyway … / …. "

IRENE: "Oh!, there! (A Decade [so to speak!])!

I have not that make me IRENE, you know ROBERT!"

ROBERT: "... / ... May anyway regain Latin America, more or less suitable manner; and more or less clean!"

IRENE: "I really have nothing to do me! If only he knew! Alberto Rodriguez if he knew; he only had to behave towards me; and so, he certainly; certainly! That's all: Certainly!, would not have to know the fate that is being know now!"

ROBERT: "I totally agree with you! That's all agreed!, indeed! But that does not prevent him A. RODRIGUEZ cans anyway go home with a more suitable outfit! Otherwise."

IRENE: "Otherwise?"

ROBERT: "Otherwise, he would give even more trouble, to his mother, whose the husband had died there not long time ago, following a plane crash!"

IRENE: "It is true that for his father; for "his late" father – there, quite frankly, I am very, very sad! Very, very sad! That's all very, very sad! And even his mother, who is now a widow, it's really sad! Very, very sad! That's all very, very sad too!".

ROBERT: "This is in order to spare his mother the implications of this case RODRIGUEZ; which might, for example, to treat her, unpredictable and incalculable consequences!"

IRENE: "Verily! That's all verily!, ih!, ih, ih!"

ROBERT: "That's why his son Alberto RODRIGUEZ simply would need "two little Sanctimonious" of United Civilians: the Birth of the little Elisio RODRIGUEZ GOMEZ and "the Certificate of Acknowledgment of Paternity" that her dad had commissioned at the Town Hall; which it obviously; obviously! That's all: Obviously!, has a copy. And therefore!".

IRENE: "And then?"

ROBERT: "And therefore to your request; that is to say, at the request of the mother you are: another double one remake (7) { : *Double of the "Certificate of Acknowledgment of Paternity", from this Copy that is at the City Hall.* }!"

IRENE: "Let me go and ask for Alberto Rodriguez, the two State – Civil Paperwork! Which ones, he asked me?"

ROBERT: "Or at least one of two! The key is that we end up indeed, that's all indeed!, agreed!, the name of the father; that is to say: the name of RODRIGUEZ! But otherwise, all "these two Certificates" are preferable for him!".

IRENE: "But! He is "foolish, foolish ally", this Alberto RODRIGUEZ!".

ROBERT: "And why is he "delirious"?".

IRENE: "But it was indeed; that's all agreed!, indeed!, himself had destroyed them, eh! And now he's asking the same State Civil Papers – there! He had only: do not rip and burn them!".

ROBERT: "He knows himself RODRIGUEZ. When he had acted in this way as a result of uncontrolled anger! And immediately after this, in the bottom of himself, he was very, very strongly regretted his rather inhuman gesture! In addition, he hardly knew, he did not go immediately to need these Official Documents exactly! Exactly! That's all exactly! What heap of paradox!"

IRENE: "So what?"

ROBERT: "So, now that really need these Documents; we implore you, the mother of ELISIO to go ask for him: not the Original; but only the Duplicate from these Copies; which Copies are archived in the City Hall of "District" where was born this little ELISIO exactly! Exactly! That's all exactly!".

IRENE: "So then, my dear Robert MERYC, I'm really sorry! I'm really sorry! I'm really, really sorry to let you hear: "That he gonna long wait! Long! Very, very long 8 { : *"I'm really, really sorry to let you hear:*

That, he will wait "so to speak: till the Greek calendars"!

That, he will wait "so to speak: till to postpone up indefinitely "

That, he leaves wait virtually until the end of the world! ".

That is to say, anyway?

This is to say that just Alberto RODRIGUEZ waits "two small State — Civil Sanctimonious", until a time that will never happen at all at all!

Why?

It is neither more nor less, because Greek months have hardly any, calends;

which they are found among the Romans;

or rather to express it more precisely: calends which they were found in "Romans" in ancient times especially; to mention only that period!

Finally, let's be more serious now!

I do not want to help ALBERTO!

I refuse to make that move!", would very, very explicitly explain Miss Irene LUCINDAÇIO, at Robert MERYC. }; if he counts on me Irene LUCINDAÇIO, to go any slightest gesture in his favour! Anyway, it's out of the question!". In any case, it's the least I can tell you ROBERT!".

Robert MERYC: "Finally! I'm there, that you pass only; or at least I'm there, that you try to convey the message of himself Alberto Rodriguez asked me to convey to you huh!!!"

Irene LUCINDAÇIO: "Ih! Indeed! That's all indeed!, agreed!, I know! Agreed! That's all agreed!, indeed!, I know.

I know that in every way, you ROBERT, you're there for nothing in this case which concerns me IRENE and him ALBERTO! You're only a stranger in this case! You're there for nothing! But as to him Alberto RODRIGUEZ!

He knows only in summary: he would never, ever, hope that I IRENE, I will make him any size magnanimous gesture!"

ROBERT: "Hence, it is left with more than twenty – four hours; hour to hour; in order that he be sent "then these Official Documents" in the Police Station where he finds himself; or even send them to his Lawyer; once again with yet, here is her address: "527 New Bond Street London W 1Y 9 DD"; and whose telephone number is: 00 – 11 – 22 – 33.".

IRENE: "Just a second! Since you insist so much! So I'm going to get a piece of paper and a pencil; in order to record them anyway: and then go directly, to a store these details right place, so it does not get lost! The story to make you happy!"

ROBERT: "It's very nice of you IRENE!"

"... / ... That my decision ... / ... is and will always be: constant; immutable and irreversible! "... / ...". In this case, it would be: "The Other Form Of Torture Of Your Own Conscience"!"

Then a few seconds later, Irene LUCINDAÇIO says: "Go ahead!". And therefore she would be given the coordinates of Lawyer of Alberto RODRIGUEZ. Then IRENE would repeat to ROBERT: "I have anyway, in spite of myself, referenced these coordinates to the form; and above all, to make you happy; it is hardly to disappoint you. But only now, I'm telling you right now; or rather, I'm telling you right now, I would not do anything to make the deadlock Alberto RODRIGUEZ! On the contrary, if I could do something to further worsen the situation; if I could do something to sink more and more that RODRIGUEZ! Anyway, I would not hesitate one small second, to actually do so!"

ROBERT: "IRENE?"

IRENE: "Ih!, Yes, ROBERT! That's all right yes!"

ROBERT: "I do not impose anything on you! That is to say: I do not push you to "definitely help him"! And I will not stop you either, to do that!".

IRENE: "I know! You all you do is: send me a message; which message you received from him Alberto RODRIGUEZ!"

ROBERT: "You yourself, you are (1) { : [As they say!]. }: "Your freewill". And consequently, you know very well; very well! That's all: Very well!, what you gonna do! I, as you have rightly pointed out, I'm just carrying the message that was entrusted to me you! But as to whether you want my opinion IRENE!".

IRENE: "Yeah! That's all yeah!, ih!, ih, ih! I would love to hear it anyway, just to know eh! And this is not binding at all to something!".

ROBERT: "Of course! Of course! That's all: Of course!".

IRENE: "Because it really turns out to be useless to repeat it for you again once more ROBERT, like what, my decision about any goodwill gesture; any act of favour vis-à-vis RODRIGUEZ, is: "NIET!" ["No!"]. And remains; and will always be: constant; immutable and irreversible!".

ROBERT: "I know very well; very well! That's all: Very well!, since you've told me and repeated it to me, several times!".

IRENE: "But?".

ROBERT: "But I give you my opinion anyway; which, I repeat once again that you are not obliged to follow!".

IRENE: "I'm listening!".

ROBERT: "I Robert MERYC, I would advise you to grant this ultimate aid for such.".

IRENE: "For as?".

ROBERT: "Because no matter how, it would still be expelled from Britain! But at least.".

IRENE: "But at least?".

ROBERT: "But at least he can be " properly"! This is because, if you do not do that!".

IRENE: "Surely! That's all surely!, ih! This is because if I do not do that?".

ROBERT: "It's because if you do not do that! And Alberto returns "as a true own evil", for example!".

IRENE: ""As being a true own evil", for example? Aye!, ih? That's all aye, ih?".

ROBERT: "His mother, who is already "sufficiently proven" like that, would suffer greatly! And could even this time 'it.".

IRENE: "And this time could even 'one?".

ROBERT: "And might even this time 'it, "die" outright, for example!".

IRENE: "So what?".

ROBERT: "So, if she dies ... / ...!".

IRENE: "Yes! That's all right yes!, Ih!, ih, ih! If she dies?".

ROBERT: "And if she dies! Alberto Rodriguez also could "die"!".

IRENE: "I'm sorry to put it that ROBERT; but, I could hardly stop myself at all to ask the question; or rather to better express it myself:: "So what?".".

ROBERT: "And then at that point!".

IRENE: "I listen! At that time?".

ROBERT: "At this moment all your life! Or to better express it myself: all the rest of your life, you could for example have to ... / ...!".

IRENE: "I could have use?".

ROBERT: "You could for example have to "suffer with your own consciousness"!; *"suffer with your own consciousness"!! That's all: "Suffer with your own consciousness"!,* In this case!".

IRENE: "Aye – aye! That's all aye – aye!, ih!, ih, ih! I listen: In this case?".

ROBERT: "In this case, it would be: "The Other Form of Torture Of Your Own Conscience"!".

IRENE: "Do you really think so?".

ROBERT: "I do not think so! But I have the firm belief! Firm certainty; certainly! That's all: Certainly!, due so to speak.".

IRENE: "A firm certainty; certainly! That's all: Certainly!, due so to speak?".

ROBERT: "Due so to speak, a kind of premonition that I finally, feel inside myself! That's why!".

IRENE: "It is for this?".

ROBERT: "It is for this that: "I feel so relieved myself of this kind of burden, that I might have in me, when I saw you, for example", ... / ...!".

IRENE: "Yes ih! That's all right yes!, ih, ih! Seeing me for example?".

ROBERT: "Seeing you for example later, "suffering" of the impact of this case; which begins with Rodriguez, now! From where.".

Irene LUCINDAÇIO: "Where?".

Robert MERYC: "Where this obligation, I have in me to make you this "kind of revelation that I finally, felt" in me ROBERT!".

IRENE: "Thank you my dear Robert, for thinking about me at this point! But.".

ROBERT: "But? ".

IRENE: "But, as I have already said and repeated several times for you ROBERT: I will do nothing at all, at all, to be able to save so little bit, the fate of RODRIGUEZ! And I repeat that "my decision is and will remain: constant; immutable and irreversible"!".

ROBERT: "IRENE?".

IRENE: "Ih!, Yeah!, ROBERT! That's all yeah!, ROBERT!".

ROBERT: "Listen to me very well! Very well! That's all: Very well! Everyone you tell me there! I understand you very well! Very, very well! That's all: Very, very well! And there is no doubt about that!".

IRENE: "But?".

ROBERT: "But I would ask you just to understand me and as a result, do me a favour!".

IRENE: "How?".

ROBERT: "By talking directly yourself on the phone! That said, in order to qualify course my words! Of course! That's all: Of course!... / ....".

IRENE: "Uh – huh! That's: Oll: Uh – huh!, ih!, ih, ih!".

ROBERT: "If you, yourself, for example you answered directly; and especially if you answered very, very exactly, that's all, very, very exactly, the same way that you respond to me ROBERT now; if you yourself would answer directly, to "your Adam"; or rather to "your ex – Adam" Alberto Rodriguez, as you are about to answer to me now!".

IRENE: "Righty – ho! That's all, righty – ho!, ih!, ih, ih!".

ROBERT: "Here's the phone number of the Police Station where he finds himself. This is the ... / ....".

IRENE: "Wait me a minute to get a pen and paper to write it down!"

ROBERT: "Righto! That's all, righto!, of course! I wait!".

IRENE: "That's it! Go there now, I'm ready!".

ROBERT: "So this is: 1 – 2 – 3 – 4 – 5 – 6 – 7 – 8.".

IRENE: "It's easy! It is well noted!".

Robert MERYC: "And you ask to speak with the "expelled"! Because no matter how Besides, "your ex – parishioner Alberto RODRIGUEZ" turns out to be (in his own words on the phone), ""the only individual so to speak": "deportable" and "expelled"" finding himself at the Station of "Broadway London SW 1 HOB D."!".

IRENE: "Thank you my dear Robert MERYC, for giving me your opinion on this matter!".

ROBERT: "You're welcome!".

IRENE: "Frankly!".

ROBERT: "By all means! That's all, by all means!, ih!, ih, ih! Frankly?"

IRENE: "Quite frankly, your opinion finally, made me working my brains!".

ROBERT: "Oh!".

IRENE: "Of course!, ih! Of course! That's all: Of course! Frankly, although I always pray "the Virgin Mary", for such an event, for example, may finally, get to Alberto RODRIGUEZ! Someone who made me drool the way which I suffered!".

ROBERT: "It ah!".

IRENE: "Although my family such as, " had worked quietly, in the same sense there; and this, in a rather Mysterious way" and "Irrational", so that the greatest misfortunes, reach "as a hominid", as demonic, it is that Alberto RODRIGUEZ!".

ROBERT: "Oh! Your family did that?".

IRENE: "And how!".

ROBERT: "It's really unthinkable huh!, in these days, it can still be done in Civilized countries, as was done in medieval times, for example!".

IRENE: "And yet, my family was actually well thought out and even made! We should not forget ROBERT, such as my parents, are from the countries where fetishes are fashionables!".

ROBERT: "And be it! I have not heard anything; and I said nothing eh!".

IRENE: "Even if you tell him, for example! I do not care passionately!".

ROBERT: "No, I will hardly do that; especially as it would further complicate the things!".

IRENE: "Well, quite Frankly, all those you have called me, though it is then that of your own opinion! ".

ROBERT: "But?".

IRENE: "But all of them give me anyway eventually, many troubles! Especially what makes me more sad is this news of the death of his father; this business that "the Company's BEUSCHERILVA" "Import – Export": this businessman, is also involved in the sale of raw coffee, between – others in England!".

ROBERT: "And okay! That's all Okay!, it was himself "Sir" Eliodoro RODRIGUEZ, the father of Roberto Rodriguez, who was the boss! And "this guy" is dead, there are three months!".

IRENE: "Eliodoro RODRIGUEZ which, I admit (2) { *: "It really is the case to express it!", she would say, to him.* }, thanks to some of his "asset" Alberto Rodriguez had obtained some of the transactions here in Europe; he had bought me a house, at home, in Portugal, and in particular on the island of Madeira! He also paid me the full cost of the driving school for obtaining a driving license, and at the same time he bought for me "a nice BMW car, brand new!". And this ALBERTO who later would become "a real manure", bought me "so many other things", I do not actually know you ROBERT list here!".

ROBERT: "It really is, as you expressed yourself IRENE: this is the case to say it!".

IRENE: "His dad Eliodoro died! Eliodoro RODRIGUEZ who even came here three times in England when I IRENE, I was still living with him Alberto RODRIGUEZ!".

ROBERT: "Aye! That's all aye!, he's dead!".

IRENE: "He admired me a lot, as if I too was "his own bitch!"."

ROBERT: "And aye – aye! That's all aye – aye!, ih! He is dead!".

IRENE: "This businessman during the three times he came to London when I was with his son ALBERTO ... / ...".

ROBERT: "Very well!, ih!, ih, ih! Very well! That's all: Very well!".

IRENE: "He filled me presents; and he even he wanted!".

ROBERT: "And he even he wanted?".

IRENE: "He even wanted me to marry his boy ALBERTO, as soon as possible! And ... / ...!".

ROBERT: "And what?".

IRENE: "And that, I give him a lot of small children, living together with his offspring! Anyway, he was really nice vis-à-vis me; and it's really the least we can say about him!".

ROBERT: "It! You can say that!".

IRENE: "He was nice, especially since I, who was scared, he always drives me from the life of "blood"; or rather, that he says for example, "his surgeon ALBERTO" to leave me; since I had ... / ....".

ROBERT: "Since you had?".

IRENE: "Since I had a boy who was already a little big anyway, at this time; Alberto RODRIGUEZ which was not even the parent!".

ROBERT: "But?".

IRENE: "But "I was very copiously; copiously! That's all: Copiously!, surprise", he did not tell me anything at all about it!".

ROBERT: "Amazing! That's all amazing!".

IRENE: "No, no! There was nothing said at all!".

ROBERT: "Did he at least saw the son in question?".

IRENE: "Many times the same! And he had also paid him considerably; *considerably! That's all: Considerably!*, presents!".

ROBERT: "Did he know at least that he was not little, of ALBERTO?".

IRENE: "Of course! Of course! That's all: Of course! Not only that his heir ALBERTO had told him more than once! But also, myself also, I'd told him repeatedly!".

ROBERT: "There is no doubt: he was very good as daddy.".

IRENE: "Or as a stepfather to me eh! And that you can say absolutely! Absolutely! That's all absolutely!".

ROBERT: "I, quite frankly, I had never, ever, had the opportunity to meet him! ALBERTO spoke of him simply; and that, on several occasions.".

IRENE: "And that man! Is he dead?".

ROBERT: "Absolutely! Absolutely! That's all absolutely! This is "a crash of a private jet", which there was unfortunately, alas!, no survivors!".

IRENE: "Good! Anyway my dear Robert MERYC, much has been done; and I am very, very happy; That's all very, very happy, to talk with you. And now I am in this obligation to cut, or at least for the moment!".

ROBERT: "Obviously! That's all Obviously!".

IRENE: "And so I'll let you know what I can do ROBERT.".

ROBERT: "OK! That's all OK!, IRENE!".

IRENE: "Goodbye ROBERT and soon. ".

ROBERT: "Goodbye IRENE.".

"Better be ashamed; which happen fast! Rather than having to endure: "The Other Form ... / ...."! That it does not happen and consequently; *and consequently! That's all: And consequently!, remains, forever, with you and with her, its many unpredictable consequences ... / ...!".*

Immediately after, Robert MERYC telephoned the Police Station; he telephoned the Office of the "R. Neville" (or rather: the Police Station "The King Maker" ["The King Builder"]), which was guarded Alberto RODRIGUEZ; that is to say, after chatting long, long time on the phone with Irene LUCINDAÇIO (and for good reason). But curiously, curiously! That's all: Curiously!, no one picked up the handset. Finding himself so needy final urgent in favour of ALBERTO course; of course! That's all: Of course!, ROBERT insisted until fifteen attempt; but only here, there was always someone on the phone.

And at the sixteenth attempt, it sounded: "busy".

He continued to insist again until eleven again; but "always busy".

Really, it was not at all, at all likely to RODRIGUEZ, in that case concerning himself.

However, Robert had decided to drop outright; he had "thrown in the towel". The main thing for him; or to be able to express more correctly: the key to his conscience was now: at least he had well and truly delivered the message. So as to know about the events, he did not want to insist everything.

Then suddenly, his phone rang. We had called him home.

And it was from that?

Robert MERYC he had initially thought it was unquestionably Alberto Rodriguez himself who, by dint of a long wait; very long time; long, long time, the phone call from him (1) { *: From him, Robert MERYC.* }, had consequently; *and consequently! That's all: And consequently!,* only the preferred (2) { *: Remembers Robert MERYC.* } to remind himself to know, after the telephone conversation, if not: following the very, very long phone conversation that he "would have had"; if and only if he had; that is to say, with IRENE.

In fact, it was the call from the by whom? That's all right: AYE – AYE!: In fact, it was the phone call from whom?

In reality, it was IRENE, who had called ROBERT.

She would tell him what?

This one seems to ROBERT: "After thinking well, I preferred to seek advice by telephone from my Lawyer, Master Gamal CHAUVRY; which had me out of this unfortunate affair "engineered" by "the conspirator" Alberto RODRIGUEZ!".

ROBERT: "You had been on the phone? And what he had advised you?".

Irene LUCINDAÇIO! " Fortunately; *fort fortunately! That's all: Fort fortunately!,* as it is night; he was present at his house!".

ROBERT: "And what did he say?"

IRENE: "I want you to immediately point out that I had the opportunity to ask for advice by phone to some other, our friends (3).". { : *I would say over there, friends of Alberto Rodriguez also! ", would say Irene LUCINDAÇIO. ".* }.

ROBERT: "And what do they all had advised you?".

IRENE: "Everybody said to me ... / ...!".

ROBERT: "All say to you?".

IRENE: "All told me basically, and of course, of course! That's all: Of course!, to each his words, but basically [I quote]: "But IRENE! You become "fada" or "paranoid" or do we know yet another, or what? But open your eyes very well; very well! That's all: Very well!, and you will understand! How can you accept finally, to get for him "such formal sanctimonious"?

You do not know if he procures thou; and those he received prior to the expiration of the time that he was leaning; we will no longer deport all!

Hence, it would be more truly, to give him "a reasonable time before expulsion", as he believed lie to you (4) { : *Indeed; that's all indeed!, agreed!, it was a strategy of Alberto Rodriguez, in order to benefit any leniency from L. IRENE.* }!

We'll just release him so he also could take care of his child (5).
{ : *Whose IRENE had managed successfully to make naturalized "British citizen" for being born, in English soil.* }.

So IRENE!

Tell us only, after all the troubles that this "sadistic" could make you suffer!

Making you even enter, "until jail" for nothing!

And you'd just forget; and therefore continue to relive with him as before?

Admit it you?". [End of quote].

Everyone told me like this, everyone's language, as I said at the beginning! And I answered ... / ...!".

ROBERT: "And you answered?".

IRENE: "And I answered: "No ohn!, ohn! Not ohn! No, no!". Then, I then decided to call directly Alberto Rodriguez himself at the number: 1 – 2 – 3 – 4 – 5 – 6 – 7 – 8, which one you gave me; to talk to him myself alone; and this without any complacency: certainly not! Thus, there is not a long time, we had chatted for more or less long!".

ROBERT: "Ah! That is to say, when I phoned him; and it sounded "busy"! It was with you IRENE that he conversed?".

IRENE: "It is quite possible! But anyway, I told him very systematically, very systematically! That's all: Very systematically!, that it was indeed; that's all indeed!, agreed!, himself Alberto Rodriguez, who had torn and even burned the originals of these two Civil Status Papers! And further, that it was indeed; that's all agreed!, indeed!, him, despite the fact that he had Officially recognized the child; that is to say: Elisio GOMEZ RODRIGUEZ, who has more, so to speak, followed by almost all physical traits of her Dad ALBERTO! But unfortunately, alas, he still continued to deny her!".

ROBERT: "Hence?".

IRENE: "Hence, I told him that I did not have to help him! And besides, I did not have time to go in the morning at the City Hall to ask the Duplicates of these Documents; it is because I respected "my household work"; which became now as.".

ROBERT: "As being?".

IRENE: "As being neither more nor less, "my son of Adam"; as now: no more, no less "my beloved Adam" simply!".

ROBERT: "Aye! That's all aye! Aye – aye! That's all aye – aye!, I understand you very well! Very well! That's all: Very well!".

IRENE: "However ... / ...!".

ROBERT: "It is?".

IRENE: "But even if I have, as is indeed; that's all agreed!, indeed!, the case, a cut, enter schedule morning and evening ... / ...!".

And one on of the best. And just happens to Aminata Ayichatoune of "Mali" is exactly; exactly! That's all exactly!, the same.

ROBERT: "Surely! That's all surely!, ih!, ih, ih!".

IRENE: "I bluntly told him that even if I have the moment between the time of morning and evening; but ... / ...! ".

ROBERT: "But?".

IRENE: "But there is no way that I could help him, so slightly! It is crystal clear that I refuse; I always refuse, to undertake such steps. I always refuse, whatever the supplication that "this sadistic Alberto Rodriguez", make to me!".

ROBERT: "And you told him yourself, by your person obviously! That's all: Obviously!, on the phone?".

IRENE: "And how! But of course I've always said! Of course! That's all: Of course!".

ROBERT: "And what he told you?".

IRENE: "He supplemented me as a kid. He implored me. Maybe even a child cannot even implore his mum, that way, so she gives him candy, for example! He told me to excuse him; and

that if he continued to deny his own child Elisio RODRIGUEZ
GOMEZ ... / ...!".

ROBERT: "Obviously! That's all Obviously!, ih!, ih, ih! ".

IRENE: "It was supposedly: because I, after " I nestled" only two
days together with him; but however, without going so far as to
consult a gynaecologist for example, to investigate a possible
pregnancy; I had, however, declared to him: that I was already
conceived!".

ROBERT: "Ah!, I see what you mean to me! Alberto Rodriguez
had not appreciated what was yet a mere joke! Is that right?".

IRENE: "A simple joke! Hum mm! It was a reality eh!".

ROBERT: "You told him that, after only two days?".

IRENE: "Oh I see! You also amaze you, we would tell you huh?
Finally, you "the hominids", you are almost all the same eh!".

ROBERT: "It's not that!".

IRENE: "But?".

ROBERT: "That is to say, eh!, eh, eh ... / ...!".

IRENE: "One would say that Rodriguez had not even told you
about it! Hence your astonishment!!!".

ROBERT: "I must not!".

IRENE: "And yet he never, ever, never, ever; and never, ever, never, ever, stopped at all to resume everywhere that: me IRENE, I was "a nice – by – night"; as: How is [according to him!], that after only two days that "one has slipped under the sheets together with him"; and I can already hear her leave I had one, now to be already conceived!

I told him that; since in one: it was the truth! Of two: in the saying; I expressed myself in fact, with the joyous words of love eh! Believing that these words would just make him happy!

But it so happened that I was heavily slip up me! If I could tell by his reaction in advance; in any case, I was not going to tell to him anything after two days! I was just going to wait, as is logical in the state of the art before to break him the news pretty; and so, it was going to have little problem with this example! It was really just, the joyful words of love eh!

But only here, including Alberto RODRIGUEZ yet its primitive impulses drive him quite often: that one starts as it were, for example, "in amorous postures", "the most sulphurous"; he turns out to be surprisingly "one would say": "a boy who could not care less the joyful words of love!".

Finally, either!

Frankly, it sounds like you let me hear, that: RODRIGUEZ did not even mention it! Hence, does your amazement!".

ROBERT: "No, he did not tell me this story before! I had never, ever, never, ever; and never, ever, never, ever, heard this story before!".

IRENE: "Hence, your wonder what!".

ROBERT: "Absolutely! Absolutely! That's all absolutely!".

IRENE: "And as a result of these joyous words of love:

""That's all right: AYE – AYE!" "It's been a long time, he Alberto RODRIGUEZ, he never, ever, never, ever; and never, ever, never, ever, stops; never, ever, never, ever; and never, ever, never, ever, to call me a bitch!

""That's all right: AYE!" ""It's been a long time, I feel in this ultimate obligation to stop counting the number of times he treats me "the horizontal"!

""That's all right: Indeed!, agreed!" ""It's been a long time that, he Alberto RODRIGUEZ, he never, ever, never, ever; and never, ever, never, ever, stops; never, ever, never, ever; and never, ever, never, ever, to deny his own kid Elisio RODRIGUEZ GOMEZ!

""That's all right: Agreed!, Indeed!!" ""It's been a long time, I feel in this ultimate obligation, to stop counting the number of times that, he Alberto RODRIGUEZ, he never, ever, never, ever; and never, ever, never, ever, stops; never, ever, never, ever; and never, ever, never, ever, to deny his own child Elisio RODRIGUEZ GOMEZ!

""That's all right yes!;"" and yes; that's all right: Agreed!, indeed!" "" It's been a long time, that he Alberto RODRIGUEZ, he never, ever, never, ever; and never, ever, never, ever, stops; never, ever, never, ever; and never, ever, never, ever, to use again and again always the same words, to better vilify us!

""That's all right: YEP!" ""It's been a long time, I feel in this ultimate obligation, to stop counting the number of times, that he Alberto RODRIGUEZ, he never, ever, never, ever; and never, ever, never, ever, stops; never, ever, never, ever; and never, ever, never, ever, to use again and again always the same words, to better dishonour us!

""Surely! That's all surely!" ""Or indeed, that's all indeed!, agreed!, if it's a long time, I feel in this ultimate obligation, to stop counting the number of times, that he Alberto RODRIGUEZ, he never, ever, never, ever; and never, ever, never, ever, stops; never, ever, never, ever; and never, ever, never, ever, to hurt us again and again always morally and even physically; is: no more; or less; because I'm there, as a gesture of greatness magnanimous towards him RODRIGUEZ exactly! Exactly! That's all exactly! Hence, I have done enough! I have given enough!

""That's: Oll Korrect!" ""So eh!, ROBERT!

""That's all correct!" ""You see me even make a gesture of greatness magnanimous towards RODRIGUEZ?

""That's all right: OK!" ""You see me again ROBERT, do even pretend to be afflicted by example, by his expulsion announced?

""That's all right: OKAY!" ""Not ohn!

""That's all right:" ""Ohn not me!

""That' all right: HUH – HUH!" ""Ohn not me IRENE!

""That's all right yes!" ""Ohn not me Irene LUCINDAÇIO!

""That's all right yeah!, and yes!" ""Or to put it better myself: No more ohn!, now with me Irene LUCINDAÇIO!

""That's all right yes!;" "and yes!" ""If I had told to him that; if I had told to him these joyous words of love; it is because I had felt "a kind of dazzling sensation" in me, for a given, since only our second night together now; like "the same feeling" that I had ever felt with some Almeida LOURENÇO several years ago, and ... / ...!".

ROBERT: "Your former husband, with whom gave birth Ernesto DOMINGUEZ?".

IRENE: "Absolutely! Absolutely! That's all absolutely! And believe me ROBERT, that I was not much mistaken; I was going to say! Yet Almeida LOURENÇO, who listening to such a statement of my mouth was not angry! On the contrary, he was very happy!".

ROBERT: "And yeah! That's all yeah!, ih! All "the gentlemen's" do not react on the same way!".

IRENE: "Every sin that I IRENE, I had committed against RODRIGUEZ was of him to share! It was of him of "that kind of dazzling sensation" that I had known at the end of the second night only that "we are all take to one's bed" moment! It was done to make him part of what would undoubtedly ensue, undoubtedly! That's all: Undoubtedly!, "such a sensation"; believing that this would make him happy, as it once was, with "my old parishioner Almeida LOURENÇO"!".

ROBERT: "So what?".

IRENE: "So what!".

ROBERT: "Yes! That's: Oll Korrect! So what?".

IRENE: "So, Alberto Rodriguez, "son of Eliodoro RODRIGUEZ and Adelino JACINTA" (as he often used to know and telling people, and occasionally he even stated "the only son"); and then, he had never, ever, never, ever; and never, ever, never,

ever, forgiven me such things (and yet very flattering and very much in love), that I had kept after only two days we lived together. For him.".

ROBERT: "For him?".

IRENE: "For him, after only two days to find out, even if this proves to seem apparently to be true!".

ROBERT: "Surely! That's all surely!, ih!, ih, ih!".

IRENE: "For him RODRIGUEZ, me IRENE, I should be anyway, wait at least 28 days, to be finally, able to put forward such statements. Or like me I had advanced to him only after two nights of "physical link"; this is because, as I've told you ROBERT, I had felt in me "this kind of dazzling sensation", like this one do, that I had once felt; when I had "bloat" that would generate Ernesto DOMINGUEZ, there was that, a few years ago!".

ROBERT: "So what?".

IRENE: "So he would not believe me at all! Worse, he happened immediately jump to conclusions!".

ROBERT: "And "this famous gestation who had given birth to Elisio RODRIGUEZ GOMEZ!".".

IRENE: "Verily! That's all verily!, ih!, ih, ih!".

ROBERT: "Was it stayed anyway, with you, at least nine, or nearly so, from the date that you had "felt this kind of dazzling sensation"?".

IRENE: "Obviously! That's all Obviously! And you could ask him by yourself for that, you realize the truth of my answer!".

ROBERT: "Oh no! I believe you eh!, IRENE!".

IRENE: "But as to him Alberto RODRIGUEZ!".

ROBERT: "Aye! That's all aye!, ih!, ih, ih!".

IRENE: "He moving quickly to a hasty conclusion!".

ROBERT: "Aye – aye! That's all aye – aye!, ih!, ih, ih!".

IRENE: "He could only let me hear; and this very solemnly, "What" it bubbling "Fell to Earth!". And as in most, the name of Lopez Ramiro came alas!, unfortunately, unfortunately, alas! That's all: Unfortunately, alas!, in addition, to all these problems! He stopped; and ... / ...!".

ROBERT: "So, he immediately concluded that it was "a work" of Lopez Ramiro!".

IRENE: "Affirmative! That's all affirmative! He not stopped; and never, ever, never, ever, stop to think at all, 'that ELISIO would prove to be unquestionably; unquestionably! That's all: Unquestionably!, the kid of LOPEZ!

Paradoxically! That's all: Paradoxically!, and since the height of paradox that little Elisio RODRIGUEZ GOMEZ precisely, also has "the same phenotype" that he Alberto Rodriguez, the father! Namely, she has: inherited the factors directly, not from IRENE, her mom, which one, I am; but rather, directly inherited apparently ALBERTO him. ELISIO is unfortunately, not necessarily a "pretty girl" genre physically speaking anyway!; and I would have to recognize it sincerely. Instead, she has "the physical characteristic features, among – others, unfortunately": figure, so to say: "more or less atypical"; ears smaller or larger; nose more or less flattened; and it goes on. In short, she had over her biological mom that I am me IRENE: the physical characteristic features largely opposed.".

ROBERT: "In short, as the height of paradox! Not to say: the irony! The irony of fate! This small Elisio RODRIGUEZ GOMEZ therefore has also virtually the same physical characteristic traits that himself Alberto Rodriguez, the father!".

IRENE: "So now, the same father implores to me … / …!".

ROBERT: "So now, the same father implores to you?".

IRENE: "So now, the same father implores to me; he begs me: I will make him reach the Official Papers; or rather the Documents showing that he is actually the father of "a kid" that not only he does not accept the truth; but also "a kid" which one he hardly stops to bashing! Anyway.".

ROBERT: "Anyway?".

IRENE: "In any case, he should to do not expect at all, that me Irene LUCINDAÇIO, I will make for him a gesture of greatness magnanimous! In this case, he will wait a very long time!".

ROBERT: "And verily! That's all verily!".

IRENE: "In any case he annoys me greatly that case! He "the forelock" to implore me now for me to reach him the Duplicates or the Certified Copies of these two Official Documents, including himself, and yet, he had destroyed the Originals!".

ROBERT: "Whether you are throwing him achieve both Papers, or failing that, one of only two!".

IRENE: "There is no question! It's out of the question! But! But that he considers me just eh!".

ROBERT: "And affirmative! That's all affirmative!, ih!".

IRENE: "That said, I IRENE, I was very adamant with him RODRIGUEZ, on the phone! I hardly hesitated for a brief moment, to tell to him that he is downright sent off for Sao Paulo; and that, as a single parcel for example, a dot and a dash. As, at least when he was far away from me!

And so, me here in London, I can sleep peacefully!".

ROBERT: "And then he said what?".

IRENE: "After he had suggested to me, as thou me had already revealed elsewhere! And even I, finally, I asked the question in the back of myself!".

ROBERT: "What?".

IRENE: "What, "If you have not chatted you two, about all of this sacred revelation before?".".

ROBERT: "The revelation about "your conscience?".".

IRENE: "All right!, that's all right!".

ROBERT: "I swear in the name of Heaven, "Not at all!".".

IRENE: "" ME IRENE AND AN OTHER FORM OF TORTURE OF MY OWN CONSCIENCE "! ... / ...!".

ROBERT: "I swear in the name of Heaven, IRENE! "What ... / ..."!".

IRENE: "" ME IRENE AND AN OTHER FORM OF TORTURE OF MY OWN CONSCIENCE".

Hum mm!

Anyway, no, no question about that ah!

Ineffective with me IRENE!

Or to better express it in the short or medium term: no question that, with me ah!

But only here, in what could possibly affect the long term; then, I do not know absolutely nothing at all, at all "very honestly speaking!".".

ROBERT: "I ROBERT, I say, though, that it could happen to you even in the short term!

And therefore, you will not ever find peace; inner peace, I meant!

And therefore, all the rest of your life could possibly definitely become melodramatic.".

(It would be well understood that the anguish of Irene LUCINDAÇIO did not fail at all; then really: not at all, at all fail.).

The spirits warmed:

When IRENE thought that … / …:"

IRENE:"When I think of that "in the detention center", it hardly stopped us "poke"!"

""That's all right yeah!;"" and yeah!! ""It is hardly kept us "search" and we "again examine closely", supposedly: in the interest of safety!"

""That's all right: AYE – AYE!"" ""While everyone knows that these searches; so – called: to verify that it has no such item, prohibited by the prison rules things;""

""That's all right: AYE!,"" ""or even that there has been little stung by example, things "another convict";"

""That's all right: Indeed!, agreed!,"" ""are there, mostly mere pretexts to use the psychological pressure constantly exerted on the prisoners, which ones we were;""

""*That's all right: Agreed!, Indeed!!,*"" ""so that one feels considerably and completely "made discoveries"; and in practice: we feel completely and dramatically; *we feel completely and dramatically! That's all: We feel completely and dramatically!, "reduced"!*"

""*That's all right yes!;*"" *and yes; that's all right: Agreed!, indeed!*"" ""When I think "the cells»appear to be constantly; *constantly! That's all: Constantly!, searched!*"

""*That's all right: YEP!*"" ""When I think "our people»are constantly; *constantly! That's all: Constantly!, searched: How?*"

""*Surely! That's all surely!*"" ""*When I think for example that when we take you to court; you are thorough in everything twice: by going; and back!*""

""*That's: Oll Korrect!*"" ""*When I think for example that when you are sick;*""

""*That's all correct!,*"" ""*and that one sends you to the hospital: when you are searched; despite this physical state in which you find yourself!*""

""*That's all right: OK!*"" ""*Searched twice; that is to say, starting and returning!*""

""*That's all right: OKAY!*"" ""*When I think for example that as a result of this disease, yet spend time you dig, can even possibly cause you to die; and that, even before reaching the hospital;*

but your own death in itself is not at all, at all loss; rather, it is a mouth to feed in less!""

""That's all right:"" ""So there!""

""That' all right: HUH – HUH!"" ""Delving; search; search and search;""

""That's all right yes!,"" ""even if, for example, starting; or return of the court; and there are several "jail – birds»digging!»

""That's all right yeah!, and yes!"" ""And this is supposed: to be able to save time, that the search in this case, is usually limited:""

""That's all right yes!;"" and yes!, ""the pants (the "turning down»of panties, I would rather say);""

""That's all right yeah!;"" and yeah!!, ""and raise the sweater and of course: to push up the bra!""

""That's all right: AYE – AYE!"" ""But only here, and yet these gestures were for us, become "mechanicals!""

""That's all right: AYE!"" ""Were frankly speaking, not at all, at all, remained: less humiliating;""

""That's all right: Indeed!, agreed!,"" ""quite the contrary!""

""That's all right: Agreed!, Indeed!!"" ""Hum mm!""

""That's all right yes!;"" and yes; that's all right: Agreed!, indeed! ""Supposedly; Supposedly! That's all: Supposedly: In order to save time, searches were limited to panties and bras!""

""That's all right: YEP!"" ""This is to reduce us psychologically; psychologically! That's all: Psychologically!, aye!, ih!""

""Surely! That's all surely!"" ""It is vexatious constraint that we impose on inmates, aye – aye!, ih!""

""That's: Oll Korrect!"" ""Because, why, whether you are regularly subjected to successive searches;""

""That's all correct!,"" ""which coincidentally, coincidentally! That's all: Coincidentally!, they are generally limited on "than private parts"?"

""That's all right: OK!"" ""Because, why also, that such searches careful, unfortunately prevent alas!, *unfortunately, alas! That's all: Unfortunately, alas!, hardly, as "the jail – birds" do enter illegally certainly things called "banned"?"*

""That's all right: OKAY!"" ""Or even whether made to one another, of any trade;""

""That's all right:"" ""while it's very, very forbidden?""

""That' all right: HUH – HUH!"" ""However, the explanation of these painstaking excavations, proving to be elsewhere:""

""That's all right yes!,"" ""she could not, consequently, be understood that way, "a coercive submission" to the prison authority!"

""That's all right yeah!, and yes!"" ""And I'm not even talking to "the clink" of "sheet"; where one feels for example, be buried alive!"

""That's all right yes!;"" and yes! ""I do not even mention the fact that one takes time to achieve carefully weave links in the prison;""

""That's all right yeah!;"" and yeah!!, ""and thus, we would feel a lot less alone;""

""That's all right: AYE – AYE!,"" ""but only this once, even now that it just starts to feel a lot less alone;""

""That's all right: AYE!,"" ""one becomes of facto subject to be transferred at one time or another!""

""That's all right: Indeed!, agreed!"" ""And so we could move unexpectedly at any time of the night; as the day for that matter,""

""That's all right: Agreed!, Indeed!!,"" ""one asks you to prepare all your belongings;""

""That's all right yes!;"" and yes; that's all right: Agreed!, indeed!, ""one would tell to you, to mount immediately in the van;""

""That's all right: YEP!,"" ""and finally, *to be transferred into a cell of another penitentiary of "chicks"!*"

""Surely! That's all surely!"" ""And so we do not even have time to bid farewell!""

""That's: Oll Korrect!"" ""It is just a time to be able to shout for example to the attention of your immediate *neighbouring of* cells,""Hey", "the Princesses"! I cannot be with you! I transferred to one of another jail cell!"."

""That's all correct!"" ""And so, it would be the first news that will affect your old friends to one another, to walk that follows for example!""

""That's all right: OK!"" ""In fact, "the lock – up»is so to say "easy on – easy on a programmed death";"

""That's all right: OKAY!,"" ""that "the convict»is subject;"

""That's all right:"" ""and that she did not even know, for example: How do you escape?""

""That' all right: HUH – HUH!"" ""When we moved, they give you when your own snacks;""

""That's all right yes!,"" ""but we do not even have the appetite!""

""That's all right yeah!, and yes!" ""It is mounted in a van;""

""That's all right yes!;"" and yes! ""one is escorted;""

""That's all right yeah!;"" and yeah!!, ""and that, by riot Police armed to the teeth!""

""That's all right: AYE – AYE!"" ""In the van, we fit in the compartment by the establishment!""

""That's all right: AYE!"" ""And I'm not even talking about that: How can such a trip is stressful for the transferred!""

""That's all right: Indeed!, agreed!"" ""It is a journey that wants: quiet;""

""That's all right: Agreed!, Indeed!!, ""because, oddly enough, no one has actually desire to interact with anyone at all! That's all right yes!: Because, curiously, nobody really has the desire to interact with anyone!""

""That's all right yes!;"" and yes; that's all right: Agreed!, indeed! ""The looks of "jail – bird" would prove coincidentally, coincidentally! That's all: Coincidentally!, drawn toward the window of the van;"

""That's all right: YEP!"" ""where one observes sadly, the landscape shirk!""

""Surely! That's all surely!"" ""And me IRENE, I had to know all this and all that and all that, because of who?""

""That's: Oll Korrect!"" ""But of course, of course! That's all: Of course!, it was because of him Alberto RODRIGUEZ!""

""That's all correct!"" ""Hence, quite frankly, my decision is now taken; and consequently, it is impossible in any case, to take a step back!""

""That's all right: OK!"" ""Alberto Rodriguez frightened me!""

""That's all right: OKAY!"" ""Alberto Rodriguez made me very afraid!""

""That's all right:"" ""Alberto Rodriguez made me very, very scared!""

""That' all right: HUH – HUH!"" ""So eh!""

""That's al

""l right yes!"" ""So, I need absolutely free of this fear!""

""That's all right yeah!, and yes!"" ""But precisely on this: Do not they say that the best way to be able to overcome his fear; this is the face?""

""That's all right yes!;"" "and yes!" ""So my way of dealing with the very, very great fear that gave me this Alberto RODRIGUEZ; is to be now that the opportunity arises for me Irene LUCINDAÇIO, ruthless vis-à-vis that Alberto RODRIGUEZ exactly!""

""That's all right yeah!;"" and yeah!! ""Life he would end well, his career in Britain.""

""That's all right: AYE – AYE!"" ""Therefore, he will return to its soil of birth [São Paulo]; where his life into question precisely, had indeed begun.""

""That's all right: AYE!"" ""I find one, an opportunity we cannot: the best, to avenge all the troubles that Alberto Rodriguez had to endure myself Irene and the children! So no one could stop me and not even you ROBERT, with all due respect I have towards you yet!""

""That's all right: Indeed!, agreed!"" ""I found one, a golden opportunity to get back at all the atrocities that he had inflicted to me; then I take my revenge! So eh! If you have not chatted all of this sacred revelation before! Whatever! But I did spot will help! Point closed off!""

ROBERT: "I swear in the name of Heaven, IRENE "What we have not talked at all before, about this conscience!".".

IRENE: "And be it! If you lie to me, I will also say that you do not lie when your own conscience!".

ROBERT: "And what did he tell to you exactly, of course! That's all: Of course!, him RODRIGUEZ?".

IRENE: "It was suggested to me [I quote]: "You could probably sleep peacefully in London; that is to say, very far from me!".

And I wanted to hear soon afterwards, and I told him thus: "Yes ih, ih, ih!

"That's all right yes!"".

And chained [I quote]: "Quiet perhaps physically! But in any case carefully, it should be for me Irene LUCINDAÇIO, the beginning of "The Other Form of Torture!". "A Torture Of My Own Conscience"!". And on that! ROBERT you, you let me hear that you have not chatted together with him, about "this sacred revelation" "before"?".

ROBERT: "I swear in the name of Heaven, it's not! I swear in the name of Heaven, that this is "purely coincidental"!".

IRENE: "It is "coincidental" really? And "what a coincidence"? And "which coincidence" is finally, starting to leave me puzzled?".

ROBERT: "I swear IRENE, that this is "purely coincidental"!".

IRENE: "Ah! Finally is!".

ROBERT: "IRENE! Can I ask you a question?".

IRENE: "Go! And I'm listening!".

ROBERT: "With "such a coincidence" that leaves you even "puzzled" as you let me hear yourself!".

IRENE: "Obviously! That's all Obviously!, ih, ih, ih! Go ahead; I'm listening!".

ROBERT: "You do not believe 'that, eh!, eh, eh … / …!".

IRENE: "'That, eh!, eh, eh?".

ROBERT: "What you draw still change their minds by example! So … / …!".

IRENE: "To?".

ROBERT: "To help "a man of merit who" so loved you; and who gave you as gifts; some of whom, of undoubtedly! That's all: Undoubtedly!, very, very large values; it is even unnecessary to recall the nature of the presents in question?".

IRENE: "ROBERT?".

ROBERT: "Verily! That's all verily!, ih! ".

IRENE: "If we got where we have arrived today! Do you think it's my fault?".

ROBERT: "No, I did not say that! But.".

IRENE: "But?".

ROBERT: "But "a man of honour" that "his late father" also liked you very considerably; and he also gave you so many presents!".

IRENE: "I do not deny it!".

ROBERT: ""His late father" who wanted same whether you IRENE, you could get married; and that, as soon as possible, with his only son!".

IRENE: "I do not deny it!".

ROBERT: "And together, you give him a lot of small and grandchildren; unlike himself, who had only one child: ALBERTO!".

IRENE: "All that you say Robert, are true. But.".

ROBERT: "But?".

IRENE: "But it's not my fault that it went very, very wrong happened next between us!".

ROBERT: "That said! I'll still give my opinion! Go get "the two little Official Papers of Civil State; the Papers" which ones, him Alberto Rodriguez, he has asked you tomorrow from the first hour of the day; and bring them to him directly yourself; that is to say, by not leaving tomorrow morning at work!".

IRENE: "Why would I do this right?".

ROBERT: "This is so you do not waste any more time!".

IRENE: "No! I will not do that! I will not help RODRIGUEZ! In any case, there is no question of me IRENE, I help him!".

ROBERT: "And yet it should be done! Finally, this is just my personal opinion eh!".

IRENE: "But my Lawyer and some others of our friends who advised me to do exactly; exactly! That's all exactly!, the opposite! They will laugh at me!

They all wish him, to be expelled!

My Lawyer and some others of our friends all want, which expels RODRIGUEZ from England!

They hope that him Alberto, to be even expelled as soon as possible!

They even wish that him Alberto, to be even expelled today!

They even wish that him Alberto, to be even expelled now!

They even wish that him Alberto, to be even expelled presently!

They even wish that him Alberto, to be even expelled at this moment in time!

They even wish that him Alberto, to be even expelled right there!

In their opinion (and the opinion of myself IRENE way), sending him ALBERTO this could indeed; that's all indeed!, agreed!, possibly be: a real descent into the hells; similarly, it is heir to a large fortune; because it would make him a certain; certainly! That's all: Certainly!, moral injury he could never, ever, never, ever; and never, ever, never, ever, treat!

This sending him ALBERTO could indeed; that's all agreed!, indeed!, possibly be: a real descent into the hells; for all his fortune precisely, could for example, certainly; certainly! That's all: Certainly!, not to fill; and that, were it more or less undoubtedly! That's all: Undoubtedly!, voluptuously, its intimate desires; for not to say: all his bestial impulses uncontrolled; as he did with me IRENE! In short, I could not make an action for RODRIGUEZ! Since my Lawyer and some others of our friends who advised me to do exactly; exactly! That's all exactly!, the opposite! They will not understand me!".

ROBERT: "So what?".

IRENE: "So what?".

ROBERT: "Affirmative! Affirmative! That's all affirmative: so what?".

IRENE: "They will laugh at me! And I, what will do I say to them eh! And I, what I will answer to them eh!".

ROBERT: "You shall have no obligation to provide an explanation absolutely! Absolutely! That's all absolutely!".

IRENE: "I will be ashamed. I will be humiliated! That's all!".

ROBERT: "And what is it like to have such a humiliation, eh?".

IRENE: "I general against me my Lawyer and all my friends. That's all!".

ROBERT: "But after all, this turpitude will pass!".

IRENE: "I understand ROBERT, how, make yourself "the devil's advocate"! But I refuse to help him; and that's it! I refuse to help Alberto Rodriguez; and that's all! I refuse to help him; full stop! I refuse to help "the devil" and that's all; I do not want to change my decision; and that's it all!".

ROBERT: "Show up clement IRENE! Think of all the love he had shown towards you, before! Think of all the physical and numerical goods, he had procured to you of very good faith!".

IRENE: "I refuse to help Alberto and that's it all! That delivers him at home to its soil of birth [São Paulo]!".

ROBERT: "Today, you do not even measure to what degree, that despite his shots spectacular tantrums, this Alberto Rodriguez is actually a boy brave after all! You would certainly; certainly! That's all: Certainly!, never, ever, again find "another guy" like him! I prefer to tell you outright; it is because I have esteem for you IRENE! Hence, you would never, ever, never, ever, find "another gentleman" as him RODRIGUEZ!".

IRENE: "It is really pointless to try to coax me ROBERT! It really is useless to insist ROBERT! It is really unnecessary Robert MERYC, with all the respect I owe to you! And I insist on this point: It is really pointless to continue … / …!".

ROBERT: "Verily! That's all verily!, I finally very, very well cottoned your determination not to sell all of, about any positive gesture in favour of RODRIGUEZ!".

IRENE: "Ah! I'm really happy; or very happy, you finally, freelancing!".

ROBERT: "Obviously! That's all Obviously! But, I'll just repeat something to you!".

IRENE: "Go! Repeat the thing; I'm listening! ".

ROBERT: "Better be, tarnish; which happen fast! Rather than having to endure: "THE OTHER FORM OF TORTURE OF YOUR OWN CONSCIENCE"! Which, as she rightly to her, she will not pass. And consequently remain, forever, with you and with her, its many unpredictable consequences. That concludes IRENE; and thank you for phoning! Goodbye and see you next.".

IRENE: "Goodbye ROBERT.".

" ... / ... The starting point of all my misfortunes, it was the "famous perjury" myself, I had done to the detriment of Ma'am Valery GLED, wife REDLER! ... / ....".

And the total period of four working days we had granted to Alberto Rodriguez was finally, fully expired without that he could managed to get the two parts needed it badly needed. It was that way, that one had finally, been ruthlessly repressed to his home in Sao Paulo, without which neither his Lawyer; that is to say, Mistress Alcina BARBARA; nor anyone else, could not do so effectively, whatever it was, again, in favour of "the expelled": that is to say, in favour of Alberto Rodriguez, in order to stop this criminal penalty; which had weighed heavily on him.

""That's all right yeah!;"" and yeah!! ""And there: after being well heated; The Spirits were calmed down afterwards.

""That's all right: AYE – AYE!" ""And here, Irene could sleep in both ears. But for how long ?

The people who were responsible for monitoring him throughout the journey home, had given him precisely; and that, if only out of the plane of the British Company "British Air Way", on the tarmac of the airport of Guarulhos, in the hands of Brazilian authorities.

They received not only the Papers; or to better express it: the Brazilian Authorities had received the Written Records of Expulsion of RODRIGUEZ duly already translated into Portuguese (the Official language spoken in Brazil); but they received (to give them to the benefit of the "expelled", [and it was quite curious; curiously! That's all: Curiously!,] :) edible (and this is to say, a few cans and a few one rolls in bags, and some biscuits, some cheese, and cetera and so on ..., by way of supply of food, at least a day) and especially a small amount; which was not anything either; since it was a sum of thirty "Pounds" ["Pounds"], to give to the benefit of the "expelled" so that he can use for example "this tile" to make some small purchases with on the spot on his native soil.

And yeah! That's all yeah!, ih!, as there was this: several years, he had gone to England in search of an University Degree in Law; Business Law; he obviously; obviously! That's all: Obviously!, had not; otherwise he would not have to run after it; and as such, he would have it: several years he spent in England would in all, looking for an University Degree, Alberto Rodriguez was unfortunately, alas!, back, cluttering his home in São Paulo!

And once arrived home in Sao Paulo, the Brazilian authorities; which had carefully read the minutes of the "expelled Alberto Rodriguez"; they had finally, seen fit that: "He had already served quite well like that time in prison in London; and especially in the prison of WORMWOOD SCRUBS (at Wormwood Street in the eastern part of the British capital). That said, he cannot be imprisoned again from us for the same mobile.".

The Brazilian authorities had therefore immediately freed him. They released him by presenting him in turn:

not only Papers for his release;

not only all of its food supplies;

but also an even more importantly, by delivering the full ""his box"; "that is to say: thirty Pounds""; which were intended for him.

Casually, but "this yeoman" had really served; since most of these Sterling he immediately exchanged to "Cruzeiro" [SCR]; Rodriguez took a taxi in the airport of Guarulhos; taxi which brought him to his home on "Rua Olavo Fontoura, 238".

RODRIGUEZ, once actually arrived home to "fold"; and when his mom, Adelino JACINTA, had only seen him; when she saw the rather puny physical condition of his only son ALBERTO; yet when he landed, for the first time in his native land, after an absence of almost a whole decade; she would say to herself suddenly; and it aloud:

"But eh!, eh, eh!

But eh!, eh!

But hey!

But this is not true!

The son and heir of a great businessman became as a "bum"!

The son became heir as a tramp!

Crown devoted son (Project and calculations of his late father Eliodoro and myself ADELINO, his mother) to be:

""That's all right: YEP!" ""Alberto Rodriguez, "ChanceKinEmp wheeler".

""Surely! That's all surely!" ""Alberto Rodriguez, a "wheeler – guru".

""That's: Oll Korrect!" ""Alberto Rodriguez, a "business guru".

""That's all correct!" ""The heir son Alberto RODRIGUEZ, destined to be:

""That's all right: OK!" """The very symbol of success; that is to say, as was already the case for his father Eliodoro RODRIGUEZ!"!

""That's all right: OKAY!" """Which symbol of success" will begin now to work hard!

""That's all right:" ""To work hard in a Highly Competitive Environment!

""That' all right: HUH – HUH!" ""In short, the heir son destined to be "a Business Guru"!

""That's all right yes!" ""In short, the heir son destined to be "the Guru of Macroeconomics"!

""That's all right yeah!, and yes!" ""In short, the heir son destined to be "the Guru of Microeconomics also"!

""That's all right yes!;"" and yes!" ""In short, the heir son destined to be "the Guru of High Finance"!

""That's all right yeah!;"" and yeah!!" ""And today, he returns to his native land as a "bum"!

""That's all right: AYE – AYE!" ""Alberto Rodriguez became as bum!".

""That's all right: AYE!" ""It was a rude shock to Adelino JACINTA. In doing so, she herself was instantly; and never again: suddenly "fainted".

""That's all right: Indeed!, agreed!" ""She had fainted.

""That's all right: Agreed!, Indeed!!" ""She had "turned eye".

""That's all right yes!;"" and yes; that's all right: Agreed!, indeed!" ""There was very, very, very quickly phoned the ambulance.

""That's all right: YEP!" ""These being also arrived promptly; they had immediately after transported JANCITA to the hospital, including at the emergency department.

""Surely! That's all surely!" ""But alas!, unfortunately; unfortunately, alas! That's all: Unfortunately, alas!, it was anyway too late!; for not to say, far too late. Her heart, which had already become "quite fragile" because of concerns arising due to the unexpected death of her husband, had just come to let go; seeing only the physical state like tramps; state which was also pretty puny; physical state in which found her only son when he was deported from Europe.

So Alberto Rodriguez had certainly; certainly! That's all: Certainly!, seen his mother, alive; but only here, it was for just a few minutes; and he had not even been able to talk with her. He now however took over the affairs of his late father. However, the fact of the death of his mother had freaked. It was definitely a lot of trouble. Many times it was even; and he stayed out of it. He was even; and he stayed out of it; since he could not even at all, at all, stop thinking about his worries.

In doing so, Alberto RODRIGUEZ not stopped; and he did not stop to talk about some "Irene LUCINDAÇIO" to the faithful employees of the Company "BEUSCHERILVA", the Company of which he was heir; Company which was located on "Avenida Morvan Branco, 199". RODRIGUEZ, when he evoked the name of IRENE, he always did, aloud; that is to say, without, however, pop, a little. It would be so, that a night; just a few minutes before closing the premises of the Establishment of which he was now the boss (1) { *: [And for good reason].* }, Alberto Rodriguez would suggest to his two aides; that is to say: Eduardo FERNANDO and Adriano CARDOZO (2) { *: "Sir" Adriano CARDOZO; which had a small tape recorder; he started the latter, to save everything said by their young new boss.* }:

"If only "my shepherd Irene LUCINDAÇIO" in London had got me; and these, in due time, the two Papers; that is to say: of the Birth of our little girl Elisio RODRIGUEZ GOMEZ and "the Certificate of Recognition of the Child", at the Town Hall;

or, in the absence of these two Official Documents, at least one of two; I certainly; certainly! That's all: Certainly!, would pay repressed; and my mother would therefore not dead! Still continue during that time here in overseeing the Company with me, I inherited now! But me too! If I had not encountered such this beautiful young lady who was Irene LUCINDAÇIO, my mother would still be alive today! I think quite frankly; *quite frankly! That's all: Quite frankly!,* that the time has come, so I can reflect on this unfortunate accident, who had crossed my path with that of IRENE! Hence, I have to ask myself some questions to me very carefully; that is to say, my inner self:

> -Did it was not because I went where the wind took me, and drink a bottle of "Pepsi – Cola"?

And if I went where the wind took me; it was already not because I had any worries, due to people who were; and who never, ever, never, ever; and never, ever, never, ever, stopped to take "my old car V – W Ladybug Number of Series: 1300"; and this without my permission?

Which people I do not even know?

And where people might for example, to send me and indirectly, "nuts"? Speaking to me and send indirectly "in jail just"! If you look very; very well, very, very well! That's all: Very, very well!, these people had done it! They had managed to send me there twice; and this: indirectly!

And me too! If someone had offered me "this old car V – W Ladybug green" in London; and I was accepted it! Do, it was not because I had given false testimony against Madam Valery GLED, wife REDLER?

Which worked with me to "IMBOURT GUERIN – FAST – FOOD"?

And besides, that lady was absolutely! That's all absolutely!, very, very kind to me?

And I was hurt "a Daughter of Eva" like that? In order to save my honour?

Following a "blunder", and yet I had committed myself?

And as a reward, "Sir" Haman GENSEN gave me "the famous V – W Beetle"?

Which, subsequently, subsequently! That's all: Subsequently!, had cause to me, too many disasters?

Among – others: my residence permit, which was not renewed?

And making me send so initially, in prison, for a period of ten months?

Leaving, "my Fatima Irene LUCINDAÇIO" which one I loved greatly, all alone, in "this apartment two parts", located on the third floor of the "N° 122 Tottenham Court Road, London W1 (3) { : *When the young boss Alberto RODRIGUEZ pronounce these coordinates to the colleagues (Edouardo FERNANDO and*

Adriano CARDOZO, the latter of which is already recorded, and yet everything which ones their new boss said); which employees were following very, very closely, the whole message, then they would take, curiously, curiously! That's all: Curiously!, carefully noting these details and more, on the scraps of Papers.

Go find out why? }".

Leaving her all alone with nothing but her kid ERNESTO, before she give birth to our "Delilah" Elisio RODRIGUEZ GOMEZ?

Thus leaving the free one I been mad about above all in the hands of "my rival" Lopez Ramiro; which would not stop ever to call her in the Number: 7 – 6 – 5 – 4 – 3 – 2 – 1 – 0 (3) ?

And to meet the daily needs for herself and her children, "my Countess" which one I loved greatly, agreed; that's all indeed!, agreed!, to "take to bed"; and this: for almost all the time that I was in prison, with "my rival" Lopez Ramiro!

And as to me Alberto RODRIGUEZ!

At the same instead of thanking for example, "this chap then", to have supported the daily needs of the woman which one loved greatly; me Alberto RODRIGUEZ, I "beta" that I am, I preferred, because of my jealousy visceral and exacerbated; I preferred to commit multiple crimes! The consequences of which more or less fairly straightforward, are today among – others: the death of my mom!

And summary of all these; or to put it under another way: The starting point of all my misfortunes, it was "the famous perjury" that myself, I had the pleasure to be at the expense of Madam Valery Gleg, wife REDLER!

Is that true, this analysis done, I just do this in my own conscience?

And if it's true!

When he was high time to stop what I was doing; why me, I did not stop it; and therefore: confess the whole truth!

In other words, when there was still time to change my false accusation about Ma'am Valery GLED, wife REDLER!

And why I did not do that?

And now that it is indeed; that's all agreed!, indeed!, too late, I start to think twice?

That is why, to my question: "Is that true, this analysis of the facts, I just do this in my own conscience?"; so I prefer to answer with a "No!".

"No!". I prefer frankly answer: "No!".

Hence: and my encounter with Miss Irene LUCINDAÇIO, and all my misfortunes which had followed thereafter were; and are only mere chance; and therefore, they had; and they have no direct relationship with "that famous false testimony", which one I had done in London! If it could possibly relieve me, I prefer to lie to my own conscience in this way; rather than tell her the truth; truth which would make her even more difficult, in my mind exactly! Exactly! That's all exactly!".

With these remarks, the Managing Editor of Alberto RODRIGUEZ; that is to say: Eduardo FERNANDO, to reassure ALBERTO, he would repeat the words of him, turning to one in question; and he would say: "As you said boss, your meeting with Miss Irene LUCINDAÇIO; and your misfortunes that followed thereafter were; and they are just pure chance!".

And Adriano CARDOZO complements: "No boss! They did and they did (as you yourself have said boss!), No direct relationship with "the false testimony" as you did in London!".

RODRIGUEZ: "I was absolutely; absolutely! That's all absolutely!, certain, certainly! That's all: Certainly!, that it was not because of it. Thank you very much, when you reassure me that this is not because of it! You cannot imagine: How do you console me, in telling me that! In any case, rest assured me there!".

A. CARDOZO: "You know boss! When you are still a student, sometimes doing stupid things that we did not even realize! Hence, forget it!".

A. RODRIGUEZ: "Thank you. I'll think about it anymore. Although yet!".

A. CARDOZO: "Though yet?".

A. RODRIGUEZ: "Though yet my mother is well and truly dead! Died as a direct result of my misfortunes!".

A. CARDOZO: "It's an unfortunate coincidence boss!".

A. RODRIGUEZ: "My mother took care of "the BEUSCHERILVA", the Company left by my father, at his death, by the private jet crash in which he was traveling with others businessmen! But myself, if ever I was to die today, for example! To replace me at the head of the Company, inherited from my father?".

To this question, Adriano CARDOZO would reply: "But boss, you're still young!".

A. RODRIGUEZ: "Can you enlighten me please, "Sir" CARDOZO?".

A. CARDOZO: "We should think about getting married now! Like that, "the angels" who come out of this marriage, there would have obviously; obviously! That's all: Obviously!, the heirs.".

A. RODRIGUEZ: "No, no! No, I will never, ever, never, ever; and never, ever, never, ever, arrive again to love "another Rebecca"; nor, to do well anything for that matter! I no longer think now, that the circumstance of the death of my mother! "The poor"! There was seen; and that, after almost an absence of a decade; but immediately after, that is to say, before we can say "Hello!". She fell into "apples", for never, ever, never, ever; and never, ever, never, ever, to wake up! And with that, you gonna tell me about marriage! No, I never, ever, never, ever; and never, ever, never, ever, make it point to get married!".

Eduardo FERNANDO: "In this case, fortunately, there has Elisio RODRIGUEZ GOMEZ, in London!".

A. RODRIGUEZ: "Yeah! That's all yeah! There is now, only her ELISIO that, in every way!".

Adriano CARDOZO: "In that case, it would be although her mother Irene LUCINDAÇIO, we cans present the Papers she had rejected to present them, to you in London! Otherwise it would not work!".

And it was time for the finishing work that evening. The two collaborators of Alberto Rodriguez had gone home. The latter was left alone in the Establishment "BEUSCHERILVA".

Or he who, when left alone, wherever he was, he was just thinking, thinking and thinking.

But just as this mind-set, made him distracted; or extremely distracted; hence the fact that he no longer driving alone. Wherever he went, Alberto Rodriguez, had a drivers towards "the BEUSCHERILVA" who was driving.

Or indeed!, agreed!, that's all indeed!, agreed!, that night, after told long with his two collaborators, Alberto Rodriguez told his driver service, to go home, with the Company vehicle; this is because, he would still be a tiny bit in the Establishment; considerably since he had a job in his "Office". Alberto

Rodriguez told his driver that he would return home to "Rua Olavo Fontoura, 238" by taxi; and his driver, passes it back the next day to recover him and to bring him back to the work.

In truth, Rodriguez had lied. He especially wanted to take another, cars steering and drive alone to go home. That said, he left the car; he closed the premises; and he drove quietly, to especially not commit driving errors (4). { : *(And due to precisely because of its continual inattention, due to its many worries!).* }. RODRIGUEZ leaving "the BEUSCHERILVA". He ran along the "Avenida Morvan Branco". He preferred to go to "Avenida Otaviano Alves of Lima", where he was going to visit someone that he knew well, before continuing his grazes, even with him in the "Rua Olavo". A. RODRIGUEZ raning along the canal "Rio Tieté".

Barely in his way: "Avenida Assis Chateaubriand", Alberto Rodriguez would plunge into his extreme distraction of mind, due to its many problems. Then suddenly, before even getting into the "Avenida Otaviano Alves of Lima", he would lose the control of his vehicle; Alberto RODRIGUEZ would skid; he encounter the guardrail; his car would pass over it; and therefore would end its "race" in the canal "Rio Tieté". Alberto Rodriguez would be so downright out of road and back into the water. He would be trapped in his car all the time, waiting for the people who luckily saw this sad accident, can alert (5) { : *And it quickly; or as soon as possible even.* } relief; and that they come to get him out.

All of these, as had occurred very quickly. But that's only when the firemen came, it was already, already, too late: the body of Alberto Rodriguez would indeed; that's all agreed!, indeed!, be inanimate; and you could not do anything at all, at all, to bring it back to life. He had wanted to take one of the cars of management on the sly; and here is the result of race: his death (6) { *: The weeks and months following each other, "this death" had occurred in just six months exactly; exactly! That's all exactly!, since Alberto Rodriguez was discharged from the British capital. }*!

The Employees of A. RODRIGUEZ were notified for the "the deceased" of the last. In doing so, saw the new shape of things (7) { *: (And that, of course, of course! That's all: Of course!, quickly).* } events, one evening, the employees of A. RODRIGUEZ; that is to say: Adriano CARDOZO and Edouardo FERNANDO (8) { *: Which in fact, were already old, very close associates of his father Eliodoro RODRIGUEZ; and later, those of her mother Ma'am Adelino JACINTA.* }, with the coordinates of Damsel Irene LUCINDAÇIO in London, although they had obtained before; that is to say, the night of the death of their young boss Alberto Rodriguez, from the latter himself; hence, someday latter, they would come in contact by telephone with Miss Irene LUCINDAÇIO (9) { *: Irene LUCINDAÇIO which, with the invaluable assistance that had been provided by an asocial assistance; which was responsible for its delicate case; she finally, managed during those times, find another job of the "cleaning lady"; which had for her work, the schedules, which allowed her to retrieve hers children from the Services for "EWO" / "ESW"; the*

"L E" and "A C"; and that was precisely what she had also done. } in London; and to tell her (in Portuguese language, and not English speaker): the whole story, from the death of the mother of A. RODRIGUEZ.

However, they tell her that they would naturally need two Official Documents; which, Alberto Rodriguez had already asked him once, in order to ensure the legacy on behalf of "the heiress" called Elisio RODRIGUEZ GOMEZ.

Listening only the whole sorry story, IRENE said immediately: "Okay. That's all OK! That's all Okay! That's: Oll Korrect! Tomorrow morning; that is to say, from the very first time, I'll ask the two Official Papers at the City Hall. I will not go to work. I will give as an excuse: like what I'm sick; and like that, from the very first hour of the opening of the hall, I'll be there, to ask these two Papers. And like that, immediately after, I'll send them by registered mail.".

"The ectoplasm" of the suicide of ALMAIDA "would stuff she, herself" Irene LUCINDAÇIO, inflexibly enough "at the time"?

"The monomania" of the plunge of ALBERTO in "the channel" "Rio Tieté" "at the time to come", "would wolf down" again, she, Irene LUCINDAÇIO quite relentlessly?

And since it was Adriano CARDOZO who was on the phone; 'and that Edouardo FERNANDO just listened with the "telephone receiver"; the latter would say to that one: "ADRIANO! Give her the address of the Company".

And given that Adriano did not understand what his colleague said; he would say to Miss Irene LUCINDAÇIO, being on the other side of the line: "Do not leave Miss Irene LUCINDAÇIO! An instant!".

Then he would ask EDOUARDO calmly: "What you say EDOUARDO?".

Eduardo FERNANDO: "I told you to give her the coordinates of our Society; so that she cans send the Papers needed! And while I think! Specifies her that the bitch Elisio RODRIGUEZ GOMEZ is certainly; certainly! That's all: Certainly!, heiress! But she could not possibly claim to be "sitting" actually, its rights or powers at the age of majority.

And therefore, by this age, she could not sign anything; remove or anything; except, she would receive from time to time; and that, as regularly as possible, most of the time, the money orders, or bank orders, sent on behalf of her the mother, so that she takes good care of her; which mandates come from the Directors of "BEUSCHERILVA" we are.".

Adriano CARDOZO: "That is to say, on behalf of yourself and myself what!".

Eduardo FERNANDO: "It goes without saying!".

Adriano CARDOZO: "Indeed! That's all indeed!, agreed!".

Eduardo FERNANDO: "Tell her especially since I arrived in London in three days; and we'll talk about very, very deeply. Very, very well! That's all: Very, very well!".

Adriano CARDOZO: "I then told her not to send these two Official Documents that we ask her by registered mail; because, ultimately, it's not worth; because you, you go to London in three days like that, after putting the record straight with her, yourself face to face, you bring them again with you, here in Sao Paulo, what!".

Eduardo FERNANDO: "Absolutely. Obviously! That's all Obviously!".

Adriano CARDOZO: "Okay. Verily! That's all verily!".

And he had said all he had to say to Miss Irene LUCINDAÇIO. But all that night, after the phone call; which one, she had received the evening, the night IRENE would not happen to snooze (IRENE would not happen to fall asleep). All that night, she would say; and she would repeat to herself:

"–What kind of "Salome" I am me Irene LUCINDAÇIO?

I did not kill the mother of Alberto RODRIGUEZ and that, indirectly?

By refusing to go to seek the same Official Papers of Civil state; which ones I am asked today; and me Irene LUCINDAÇIO, I agree directly?

And why, I do not refuse, as I had already mercilessly refused at the time; that is to say, when Alberto Rodriguez asked me; begging me even?

I did not kill and indirectly Alberto Rodriguez himself, by dropping him into the channel?

The same Papers that I did not want to pick up! And today, I am willing to pick up them; in order to transmit the legacy to "my heir"?

What manure that I am IRENE, really?

What kind of "Penelope" am I exactly?

"A Cleopatra" who thinks only about the materials and numerical interests?

And now that I have two deaths in my consciousness!

What do I do?

(And one on of the best. And just happens to Aminata Ayichatoune of "Mali" is exactly; exactly! That's all exactly!, the same.).

By the way: How could I forget all of them fairly?

And why, I do not refuse the transfer of the inheritance in favour of "my Judith"?

Finally, is!

Finally, I forget all of them like that, tomorrow morning, I do not even would bring "the small girl" in the Nursery.

Tomorrow, I do not even go to work.

I do not even would bring "my Daughter of Eva" tomorrow morning at the Nursery; this is because, in case (10) { : *"You never, ever, never, ever; and never, ever, never, ever, know!", she would say to herself.* }, one would also need its presence!".

And Miss Irene LUCINDAÇIO tried to sleep, supposedly forgotten, until the next morning. But the problem is that all that night, it happened that: she did not happen (and then really: she does not happen at all, at all, to close the eyes; not even a tiny moment).

She certainly; that's all indeed!, agreed!, did, fortunately, for her, but think of all this fortune, which one was simply trying to transfer by that way to her own family. And it made her dizzy.

She certainly; certainly! That's all: Certainly!, did, fortunately for her, but think of all this fortune; but not only.

Not only is it because she was also, alas!, unfortunately, think that "the both dead": it was now, in her consciousness.

She never, ever, never, ever; and never, ever, never, ever, succeeded really, stop thinking.

How long it last?

Was it not already there: "THE OTHER FORM OF TORTURE OF HER OWN CONSCIENCE", which one a certain Robert MERYC and even himself Alberto Rodriguez had spoken to her before; which begins and coincidentally, alas!, unfortunately?

All these tragedies; all these disasters; … / … Were the direct consequences; the direct impact of the "untimely contest" to two circumstances: … / …

The next morning, she, Miss Irene LUCINDAÇIO, who had hardly slept at all, all the night; she is preparing to go to the City Hall, to go and ask the two Official Papers of Civil State; which we had requested. After washed; after telling to his son to wash himself; after … / …; after … / …; after washing ELISIO; after taking all the breakfast together; after "having all very; very, very well! That's all: Very, very well!; very, very, well dressed" (and after "having prepared" to exit); and after accompanying his kid Ernesto DOMINGUEZ, to the middle School; IRENE took "her pussy ELISIO"; and very; very, very well! That's all: Very, very well!; very, very, well dressed; and she had taken the wheel of her car "BMW."; to go to the City Council.

She was very good finish; and she had indeed; that's all indeed!, agreed!, got the both Official Papers of Civil State; which ones she wanted so much to get.

""That's: Oll Korrect!" ""Irene LUCINDAÇIO was so happy.

""That's all correct!" ""Irene LUCINDAÇIO was very happy.

""That's all right: OK!" ""Irene LUCINDAÇIO was very, very happy.

""That's all right: OKAY!" ""However, she wanted to be part of this very, very good news to her friend Patricia CRISTOVAO; which lived in Hyde Park 1 { *: In the Western part of London.* } IRENE had actually told to her, too, as she had expected.

That said, PATRICIA only managed to hide little lust, she had proven quite frankly now, IRENE towards her friend.

Miss Irene LUCINDAÇIO took over the wheel of her "BMW"; to return at her home, in the "122 Tottenham Court Road". She ran along the "The Serpentine Road"; and since she had not been snoozing all the night (2) { *: [And for good reason!]*. }, she had dozed just a few seconds behind the wheel.

But it was (3) { *: Unfortunately alas!* } unfortunately, alas!; unfortunately, alas! That's all: Unfortunately, alas!, very ample!:

""That's all right:" ""for her, she lost the control of her vehicle;

""That' all right: HUH – HUH!," ""for she slips;

""That's all right yes!," ""so that she strikes the guardrail;

""That's all right yeah!, and yes!," ""so that she passes over the latter;

""That's all right yes!;"" and yes!;" ""and she ends its run on ["The Long Water The Serpentine"].

""That's all right yeah!;"" and yeah!!" ""All these, were spent in full speed, "the BMW car" ended up in the water. Irene LUCINDAÇIO had made an effort to open the window and the door, to get out of the vehicle; but difficult; and to try to do, get out "her Pony" from this sad situation; and all those she had to do; it is only a few seconds while the car might continue to sink, into the bottom of the water.

But alas!, it was too many things to be taken in a short space of time.

Therefore, Miss Irene LUCINDAÇIO could hardly do anything in order to save "her" "Heir (4)". { : *[What destiny!]* }. When the firefighters – emergency personnel came there; that they could not raise only the dead body, of "a Pussy".

""That's all right: AYE – AYE!" ""The "ectoplasm" of ALMAIDA's suicide "swallowing" her, Irene Lucindacio, already quite inflexibly "at the time".

""That's all right: AYE!" ""The "monomania" of ALBERTO's great plunge into "the canal" "Rio Tieté" "at that moment again," "swallowing" her again Irene Lucindacio, quite implacably.

""That's all right: Indeed!, agreed!" ""The "ghost" of her run; which had ended "at this moment again," with a great plunge into [the] "The Long Water The Serpentine"; ensuring that "her little mommy Elisio" left her skin there, "swallowing" her again Irene Lucindacio, quite cruelly.

""That's all right: Agreed!, Indeed!!" ""And it was in this circumstance that "one of the administrators" of "the BEUSCHERILVA Company"; that is to say: "Mr." Edouardo FERNANDO, had come from Sao Paulo to London, in order to do what was necessary for the benefit of "the cracker named Elisio GOMEZ RODRIGUEZ".

""That's all right yes!;"" and yes; that's all right: Agreed!, indeed!" ""And as it happened, she had just died, "two days ago".

""That's all right: YEP!" ""Irene Lucindaçio certainly, certainly! That's all: Certainly!, would have (as for Aminata Ayichatoune) already, a boy with another Gentleman; but together with the future Businessman Alberto Rodriguez, they had planned to have a lot of "Madeira – Pão – Lista" (of Madeira and São – Paulo) [; Many kids]; according to them: some would even be able to build an air bridge between the Madeira Island and São – Paulo (in Brazil).

But only here, the fate had (as for Aminata Ayichatoune and the Professor Aziz Olenga) wanted that the things to take place differently.

Aminata Ayichatoune certainly; certainly! That's all: Certainly!, would have (as for Irene Lucindaçio) already, a boy with another Gentleman; but together with the Professor Aziz Olenga, they had planned to have a lot of "Bama – Kinois" (from Bamako and

Kinshasa) [; Many kids]; according to them: some would even be able to build an air bridge between Bamako and Kinshasa.

But only here, the fate had (as for Irene Lucindaçio and the future Businessman Alberto Rodriguez) wanted that the things to happen differently.

Brief: "The ectoplasm" of the suicide of ALMAIDA "would stuff oneself", she, Irene LUCINDAÇIO, inflexibly enough "at the time"?

Brief: "The monomania" of the plunge of ALBERTO in "the channel" "Rio Tieté" "at the time to come", "would wolf down" again, she, Irene LUCINDAÇIO quite relentlessly?

Brief: "The spectrum" of its stroke; which was over "yet – again" by a plunge on ["The Long Water The Serpentine"]; ensuring that "her little girl ELISIO" let down her skin, "ate she also" again, she, Irene LUCINDAÇIO quite cruelly.

Brief: And it was in this circumstance then, that "one of the Directors" of "BEUSCHERILVA Company"; that is to say: "Sir" Eduardo FERNANDO, had come from Sao Paulo, to London, to take action in favour of "the Chirping named Elisio GOMEZ RODRIGUEZ".

Now, she was just dead, there was "two days of that".

Brief: For Miss Irene LUCINDAÇIO, it would actually be: "AN OTHER FORM OF TORTURE OF HER OWN CONSCIENCE".

Soon after this sad affair, IRENE and her son Ernesto DOMINGUEZ, would leave Britain permanently to return home on the island of Madeira. But because she "would" and now "killed" "indirectly" and " involuntarily", at "three people", Miss Irene LUCINDAÇIO not ever stop to think about all those problems until the end of hers days.

In doing so, IRENE would become depressed; which she felt to be An Ultimate obligation to fight hers own memories; and just by fighting all these ones, this very, very charming Joan of Arc had created a small paradise in her head; which manifested herself in her apparently triggered by the frequent and most frantic, genuine confusion.

IRENE would start now, to abuse, to abuse, to abuse, relentlessly, the voices of her own conscience.

And even IRENE would be decidedly to abuse, mistreat, to mistreat inexorably, hers vocal cords. And follow it for a long period of cerebral disposition, conducted and say briskly.

""Surely! That's all surely!" ""In doing so, IRENE therefore become depressed;

""That's: Oll Korrect!," ""she would have become a great depression;

""That's all correct!," ""she would become a big neurotic depressive;

""That's all right: OK!," ""she would become a big neurotic depressive traumatic;

""That's all right: OKAY!" ""she would become a big neurotic; a big distressing; a big painful; a big devastating; a big traumatic, or post – traumatic; a big agonizing.

""That's all right:" ""-Why?

""That' all right: HUH – HUH!" ""This is simply because she would show now a secondary anxiety response to trauma; or rather, in emotional shock, which one she had received. She still had almost majority of Fortune (paid: Ten Thousand Pounds) that she had received from the judicial compensation in London; moreover, she had (1) { *: With Alberto RODRIGUEZ.* } such a beautiful and very large pavilion of herself in her country; but now opt to go to sleep outside, inside the wreckage of cars; so that she would become "dingo".

And not forget to mention the fact that, many times, in front of many simpletons, IRENE used to pronounce the names; the words and the sentences in the languages incomprehensible to those. She often told them and even their so she repeated them for them: the mornings; the midday's and the evenings; and number of times, even singing them for example, without however be shying so slightly:

(IRENE) would not stop so to speak, ever now: singing; singing; singing; singing sadly even in the air; singing nostalgically even in the air:

"Aurora;
Cãlium;
Purpurã.

Tempère;
Trõndõre;
Amarre;
Sõndõre.

Expulsa;
Rãpidãmantõ;
Quetõdã.

Diminuãwõn;
Quãntitãõn;
Fanrãwõn;
Sononrãwõn!

Alberto;
Adelino JACINTA.
Rodriguez;
Elisio RODRIGUEZ GOMEZ;
Adriano CARDOZO;
Eliodoro RODRIGUEZ;
Irene;

LUCINDAÇIO;
Edouardo FERNANDO!

RODRIGUEZ leaving "the BEUSCHERILVA".
"Avenida Morvan Branco".
"Avenida Otaviano Alves of Lima",
"Rua Olavo".
Canal "Rio Tieté".
Here = End of Life of Alberto

Secondly, the future businesswoman
Elisio RODRIGUEZ GOMEZ;
Elisio RODRIGUEZ GOMEZ, " the future businesswoman
ChanceKing (Queen) Emp (Empress)";
";
Elisio RODRIGUEZ GOMEZ, "a future wheeler guru";
Elisio RODRIGUEZ GOMEZ, "a future business guru".
Secondly, therefore, the Future Businesswoman
Elisio RODRIGUEZ GOMEZ; happened to be for
"the Blacks": "the very Symbol of Success";
"That Symbol of Success" that always sat still and
always, to work hard; In order to maintain their
Social Status; or: in order to gallop even Higher;
a Symbol of Success; which was "Playing" in "the Big Leagues";
"Courtyard" which proved that again and again and continues
to prove to be always a Highly Competitive Environment!

To go to the City Hall, to go and ask the
two Official Papers of Civil State!

And she ends its run on ["The Long Water The Serpentine"].
Here = End of Life of Elisio RODRIGUEZ GOMEZ

Elisio RODRIGUEZ GOMEZ narrowly missed to
become the Future Director of "BEUSCHERILVA".
-What miss for me Irene LUCINDAÇIO and for all my family!
Was it not already there: "THE OTHER FORM OF
TORTURE OF HER OWN CONSCIENCE".

Aurora;
Cãlium;
Purpurã.

Tempère;
Trõndõre;
Amarre;
Sõndõre.

Expulsa;
Rãpidãmantõ;
Quetõdã.

Diminuãwõn;
Quãntitãõn;
Fanrãwõn;
Sononrãwõn!".

Is it surprising in that!

Is not that IRENE had actually lost the North, no!

And one on of the best. And just happens to Aminata Ayichatoune of "Mali" is exactly; exactly! That's all exactly!, the same.

On several occasions she would walk without shoes and almost without clothes. So that her mind would be decidedly; *decidedly! That's all: Decidedly!,* the most time elsewhere; then current road and all alone, walking, IRENE would not stop again, so to speak:

laughing; laughing beast, beast, beast; laughing foolishly;

singing; sing stupid, stupid, stupid; "mentally retarded person" sing;

dancing; dancing whine, whine, whine; dancing whining;

snicker; fool, fool, fool; giggling stupidly;

of screaming; of shouting abet, abet, abet; rallying cry of loss of innocence;

to shout; to shout disgusting, disgusting, disgusting; to yell even disgustingly.

Irene LUCINDAÇIO would simply become "demented".

That's all right: AYE – AYE!"" Before becoming "brainsick"?""

""Before becoming "brainsick" IRENE "became unbalanced"."'

""That's all right: AYE!"" After "was harebrained"?""

""After "was harebrained" IRENE "became cracked"."'

""That's all right: Indeed!, agreed!"" Between "the states of craziness"?""

""Between "the states of craziness" IRENE "become", "crack – brained"."'

""That's all right: Agreed!, Indeed!"" Otherwise wrote: ""»

""Otherwise wrote:""

""That's all right yes!;" "and yes; that's all right: Agreed!, indeed!" Before "become skewed"?""

""Before "become skewed", IRENE "became out of sync"."'

""That's all right: YEP!"" After "being unhinged"?""

""After "being unhinged" IRENE "became even siphoned off"."'

""Surely! That's all surely!"" Between "the states of madness"?""

""Between "the states of madness" IRENE "became even more stamped"."'

Irene LUCINDAÇIO would continue with its awful "crackling". And in this way, she would leave such to hear all those and all these who would indeed; that's all indeed!, agreed!, "reconcile" with her:

""Everything had indeed; that's all agreed!, indeed!, started with those myself Irene LUCINDAÇIO, I had my first" "anthropoid" "Almeida LOURENÇO". And all who follow me, the devastations until that time – here (that is to say, boosted by my meeting with Alberto Rodriguez) are only workouts; or rather "the disasters" attracted to "the cataclysms" of old "latent"."

"Intrigues, in "the Micmac" for a better life, it would take much! And the body in all this! Everything happened at the "hocus". And on "family" of "sneaky shepherdess?"."

"Thanks to the many "pounds" they received from that one fact, they never, ever, find themselves; and this: long short "half – legs"."

"This game of "giving as an excuse", would prove to be for "the stealer" a highly codified ritual, "one would say". However, it needed for her, only a little: decompress at this time "indelicate"; and there was strength in her motivation!"

""These masks" "brides Church treasurers Revealed" "Surzur-Alvarez" are "time – bombs" and the very first victims, are not in fact the flock, but rather, "the hums flock treasurers"; in whom, keep coming: reduction; discouragement; annoyance; grief; "Agrippina"; and to top it all: "suicide by hanging"!"

"What a poster! "The convicts" and the kleptomaniacs. In this game, the most skilful "Fillies" would be the first honoured. And so all the family members of the "cock – sucking" (or almost all) live in the serenity; since "the Norway Lobster", she attend with "slices" in all their Difficult situations; "Difficult" ¾ "difficult" horizons "of the horizontal world"."

"This position of "the Daughter of Jupiter and Aphrodite" as such, was envied by dozens of "Crayfishes". They were at least: Ten; Perhaps two Dozen; perhaps Tens Three; Perhaps less; Perhaps more!"

"I did not know me ah! Everyone I knew was that several "amazons" wanted to be in my place, to "engage" them also to "tampering" of the body of the Church "Surzur – Alvarez"."

"And yeah!, ih! The Real "candelabra" to divert necessarily – forced! "The charming" "girls immorality" use this trick treasurers wife for reasons con finances."

"But of course, of course! That's all: Of course!, "a stilts" used to open the session to better relax the atmosphere. And the treasurer was a faithful "poor" who still did not know: -At who to give his confidence!"

"The grant "his merchant of Love"? But then, in the blindness, "this cash cow" granted it to "a Madam"."

"Actually, it's her "Groundhog" who hypnotized; and consequently; *and consequently! That's all: And consequently!*, she dictated those he had to do; and he, he had no other alternative than to go running!"

"If "recipe" would not fit in the trunk? What would become "the swimmer" and her family?"

"What would become those whose "The daughter of Jupiter and Aphrodite" was generously supported?"

"What would become of those whose "The daughter of Jupiter and Aphrodite" had graciously helped?"

""Some embezzlers" and "spoiled"?"

""The scoundrels" and "bitches"?"

""The scoundrels" and "bench"?"

""The horizontals" and "hussies"?"

""The core drills" and "itinerant 's mattresses"?""

""That's all right: AYE – AYE!" ""Now Irene LUCINDAÇIO drew, drew, drew unwanted attention of many, many loafers, to listen debited; to hear her talk;

""That's all right: AYE!" ""Now, Irene LUCINDAÇIO called, called, called, unintentionally; *unintentionally! That's all: Unintentionally!*, many penguins, to hear her talk;

""That's all right: Indeed!, agreed!" ""

Really, Irene LUCINDAÇIO cried; she shouted ugly; she shouted ugly; she shouted ugly; she cried badly wrong, treason;

""That's all right: Agreed!, Indeed!, " ""now she clamoured; she screeching rude; she hues and cried rude; she blues murdered rude; she roughly battled cry wrongly scandal;

""That's all right yes!;"" and yes; that's all right: Agreed!, indeed!," ""really, she cried; she cried stupid; she cried stupid; she cried stupid; she cried stupidly misfortune;

""That's all right: YEP!," ""ultimately she verbalized; she squalled fool; she gave tongue to fool; she expressed emotion fool; she foolishly out – cried emotionally: rubbish;

""Surely! That's all surely!," ""now, she cried; she cried sad; she cried sad; she cried sad; she cried sadly luckily;

""That's: Oll Korrect!," ""fortunate to have many, many "round" which was their happening suddenly with their families; then as suddenly disappeared with the death of "her pony ELISIO"; that is to say, before they can even have this loot in question;

""That's all correct!," ""now she whimpered; she blubbered miserable; she exclaimed miserable; she hollered miserable; she shouted miserably misery;

""That's all right: OK!," ""really, she cried; she cried painful; she cried painful; she cried painful; she cried sorrowfully: indignation;

""That's all right: OKAY!," ""ultimately she sniffled poor; she snuffled poor; she shrieking poor; she catcalled poor; she expressed feelings; she poorly: poverty;

""That's all right:" ""now, she cried; she cried melodramatic; she cried melodramatic; she cried melodramatic; she cried melodramatically: famine;

""That' all right: HUH – HUH!," ""now she weeping heavier wrongly; bawling heavier she wrongly; snivelled heavier she wrongly; blubbing heavier she wrongly: complaint;

""That's all right yes!," ""really, she cried vindictively wrongly; she cried vindictively wrongly; she cried vindictively wrongly; she cried vindictively wrong: Vengeance

""That's all right yeah!, and yes!," ""ultimately she laughed; screamed she soft; yelling she soft; uttering aloud she soft; wailing she softly;

""That's all right yes!;"" and yes!," ""she cried; she cried sullen; she cried sullen; she cried sullen; she shouted sulkily;

""That's all right yeah!;"" and yeah!," ""she Bronx cheering her; she snorting defective; she screamed defective; she sobbing defective; she tearing defectively.

""That's all right: AYE – AYE!" ""IRENE cried; she geeing; she cried; she booing; she cried; she screeching "screechingly".

""That's all right: AYE!" ""IRENE would stop as it ever, never again now:

""That's all right: Indeed!, agreed!," ""to discourse; to discourse; to discourse demonstratively;

""That's all right: Agreed!, Indeed!!," ""to discourse; to discourse; to discoursing circularly (, or to put it under another way: IRENE would stop so to speak, ever, never now, to discourse, to talk, to talk, to talk while walking often looped, often while walking in a circle , and this, apparently; *apparently! That's all: Apparently!*, without real reason, according to the perception, or rather, seen from the side of the people mentally healthy);

""That's all right yes!;"" and yes; that's all right: Agreed!, indeed!," ""to discourse; to discourse; to discourse; to discoursing for about annoyingly messy most of the time; or otherwise, if the words were ordained; it was about RODRIGUEZ and "their price of Diana ELISIO"; that people in Funchal, did not even know.

""That's all right: YEP!" ""IRENE would stop so to speak, ever, never now: talking; to speak; to speak; talking defensively in the air;

""Surely! That's all surely!," ""to speak; to speak; to speak; mechanically to speaking up;

""That's: Oll Korrect!," ""Huming; Huming; Huming; Huming lazily in the air.

""That's all correct!" ""Yawning; yawning; yawning; yawning lazily in the air.

""That's all right: OK!" ""IRENE would stop so to speak, ever, never now: singing; singing; singing; singing sadly even in the air; singing nostalgically even in the air.

""That's all right: OKAY!" ""About "just sing" IRENE suggested: "This sad song"; "This nostalgic song"; which I cooked up for you; and that I'm singing right now here precisely for example, your attention to you, that you take some of your precious time; to listen.

""That's all right:" ""You clearly; clearly! That's all: clearly explicitly!, have reason to want to listen to me; since "this sad song" precisely; obviously! That's all: Obviously!, since "this nostalgic song" precisely; verily! That's all verily!, sometimes could deter many of – you who were about to commit e.g. the nonsense huge; such me Irene LUCINDAÇIO, I have committed; not for example; or not, for example, commit them; since they can only lead the person who commits them: straight towards a total loss; or rather, since they can only lead the person who commits them and not forgetting to mention, many of these other people who had known her; and this, far and near: straight to the total loss; and it was very, very; very, very well! That's all: Very, very well!, exactly what had happened to me; what had happened to me I, Irene LUCINDAÇIO; and not forgetting: to many other of those people who skirted me; and this, with me myself; and that, from far and near.

""That' all right: HUH – HUH!" ""And for that, is it necessary that I quote the case of Adelino JACINTA; that is to say, the mother of Alberto RODRIGUEZ; that is to say, the father of "my late keel Elisio RODRIGUEZ GOMEZ"?

""That's all right yes!" ""And this "poor Adelino JACINTA" is such a part of many of these other people who skirted me; and this, by far or by near; with me myself; and this, by far; as I mentioned earlier.

""That's all right yeah!, and yes!" ""And for that, is it necessary that I quote the case of Alberto Rodriguez?

""That's all right yes!;"" and yes!" ""And for that, is it *necessarily! That's all: Necessarily!*, necessary that I quote the case of Elisio RODRIGUEZ GOMEZ, herself?

""That's all right yeah!;"" and yeah!!" ""Not ohn!, I do not even think it may be *necessarily! That's all: Necessarily!*, necessary to list all such cases. The few words found in the text of "the sad song"; in the text of "the nostalgic song"; which I cooked up for you; should very, very; very, very well! That's all: Very, very well!, widely enough, you discouraged to act as I had.

""That's all right: AYE – AYE!" ""Now, here is the essential content of the text "this sad song"; of "this nostalgic song":

""That's all right: AYE!" """... / ... A stunningly beautiful natural for me; I'm not there in reality, for nothing";

""That's all right: Indeed!, agreed!," ""then a whole series of matches, so to speak: not voluntary; and: not irresponsible on my part; or even: a whole series of matches as it deliberately volunteers and irresponsible on my part;

""That's all right: Agreed!, Indeed!!," ""lead me consequently; *and consequently! That's all: And consequently!*, this shows total loss.

""That's all right yes!;"" and yes; that's all right: Agreed!, indeed!" ""Very, very; very, very well! That's all: Very, very well!!, bad habits from me; I accelerated and consequently; *and consequently! That's all: And consequently!*, well; verily! That's all verily!, (: and this, not even for all that, I realizing it myself) my present total loss.

""That's all right: YEP!" ""A breach of trust on my part; quite a breach of trust on my part; against the people and yet of very, very; very, very; very, very well! That's all: Very, very well!, good faith, they trusted me; I accelerated and consequently; *and consequently! That's all: And consequently!*, well surely! That's all surely!, (: and this, not even for all that, I realizing it myself) my present total loss.

""Surely! That's all surely!" ""A long diversion sneaky and extended into the body of a small Christian Reformed Church, the ardent public (and a small Revivalist Church, a small Church awakened; revealed a small Church and a small Renovated Church, a small Church of Reform; ["a Church Communicated Divine"]); a small Church called: the "Surzur – Alvarez"; I accelerated and consequently; *and consequently! That's all: And consequently!*, well; very well! That's all: Very well!, (: and this, not even for all that, I realizing it myself) my present total loss.

""That's: Oll Korrect!" ""An abjection generated indeed; that's all indeed!, agreed!, by my very, very dirty fads; a sacred baseness generated indeed; that's all agreed!, indeed!, by my very, very dirty fads; I accelerated and consequently well; very well! That's all: Very well!, (: and this, not even for all that, I realizing it myself) my present total loss.

""That's all correct!" ""A leak off; too far; the very, very far, very well! That's all: Very well!, because of this sacred wilt in question; I accelerated and consequently; *and consequently! That's all: And consequently!*, well surely! That's all surely!, (: and this, not even for all that, me realizing it myself) my present total loss.

""That's all right: OK!" ""Sacred behaviour levity of manners on my part; I accelerated and consequently; *and consequently! That's all: And consequently!*, well verily! That's all verily!, (: and this, not even for all that, I realizing it myself) my present total loss.

""That's all right: OKAY!" ""A ruthless refusal on my part to try out Alberto RODRIGUEZ; that is to say, the father of "my little girl, Elisio RODRIGUEZ GOMEZ" from the deplorable situation in which he would find (: and he proves to be that I was the only person able to "extirpate" him, from this deplorable situation rightly, but that I, the wicked IRENE I am, I had consistently refused to do so); I accelerated and consequently; *and consequently! That's all: And consequently!*, well; very well!

That's all: Very well!, (: and this, not even for all that, I realizing it myself) my present total loss.

""That's all right:" ""A refusal undoubtedly! That's all: Undoubtedly!, unambiguous; severe and compelling in my hand, hardly to listen the telephone advice from a friend of ours by the name of Robert MERYC; which just advised me the advice such as: "… / … But we give him only a reasonable time, just enough time for that, all his family and friends which ones living by example, in "the Metropolis of London", come meet at the Police Station where he currently finds! And above.". A refusal undoubtedly! That's all: Undoubtedly!, unambiguous; severe and compelling to listen to them on my behalf; I accelerated and consequently; *and consequently! That's all: And consequently!,* well; very well! That's all: Very well!, (: and this, not even for all that, I realizing it myself) my present total loss.

""That' all right: HUH – HUH!" ""A refusal without qualms; immutable and that refuses to compromise on my part, do little to listen the telephone advice from a friend of ours by the name of Robert MERYC; which just advised me the advice such as: "… / … Otherwise, it would give even more trouble, to his mother, whose the husband had just died, it is no longer, as a result of a plane crash! ". A refusal without qualms; immutable and which refuses to compromise to be able to listen to me; I accelerated and consequently; *and consequently! That's all: And consequently!,* well; that's all agreed!, indeed!, (: and this, not even for all that, I realizing it myself) my present total loss.

""That's all right yes!" ""Inexorable refusal; strict and constant in my hand, hardly listen to telephone advice from a friend of ours by the name of Robert MERYC; which just advised me the advice such as: "... / ... That's able to save his mother the implications of this case RODRIGUEZ; which might, for example, to treat her, unpredictable and incalculable consequences! ".

""That's all right yeah!, and yes!" ""Inexorable refusal; rigorous and consistent to be able to listen the advice of this Robert MERYC; I accelerated and consequently; *and consequently! That's all: And consequently!*, well; that's all indeed!, agreed!, (: and this, not even for all that, I realizing it myself) my present total loss.

""That's all right yes!;"" and yes!" ""Strict refusal; absolute, absolutely! That's all absolutely!, and irrevocable on my part, do little to listen the telephone advice from a friend of ours by the name of Robert MERYC; which just advised me the advice such as: "... / ... That's why her son Alberto RODRIGUEZ would simply need to "two small Papers" of Civilian's State: the Birth of the little Elisio RODRIGUEZ GOMEZ and "the Certificate of Acknowledgment of Paternity"; that him, the dad had commissioned at the Town Hall; which it obviously; obviously! That's all: Obviously!, has the Copies – Certified – Complies! And therefore! ... / ...!". Strict refusal; absolute, absolutely! That's all absolutely!, and irrevocable listen to them on my behalf; I accelerated and consequently; *and consequently! That's all: And consequently!*, well, that's all agreed!, indeed!, (: and this, not even for all that, I realizing it myself) my present total loss.

""That's all right yeah!;"" and yeah!!" ""A rigid refusal; inflexible and without hesitation on my part, to do little to listen the telephone advice from a friend of ours, by the name of Robert MERYC; which just advised me the advice such as: "You yourself, you are [as they say]: "... / ... "Your free will". And consequently; *and consequently! That's all: And consequently!*, you know very well; very, very well! That's all: Very, very well!, what you gonna do! I, as you rightly said, I'm just carrying the message that was entrusted to me, for you! But as to whether you want my opinion IRENE!". A rigid refusal; inflexible and plainly to be able to listen to me; I accelerated and consequently; *and consequently! That's all: And consequently!*, well, that's all indeed!, agreed!, (: and this, not even for all that, I realizing it myself) my present total loss.

""That's all right: AYE – AYE!" ""A rough denial; systematic and irreversible my hand, hardly listen the telephone advice from a friend of ours, by the name of Robert MERYC; which just advised me the advice such as: "... / ... But at least he cans be "properly"! This is because if you do not do it!". Advice which just advised me by example again: "His mother is already "quite proven" like that, she would suffer greatly! And could even this time 'it ....". Advice which just advised me for example again: "And might even this time 'it, "die outright, for example"!". A rough denial; systematic and irreversible listen to them on my behalf; I accelerated and consequently well, that's all agreed!, indeed!, (: and this, not even for all that, I realizing it myself) my present total loss.

""That's all right: AYE!" ""A bitter refusal; categorical and relentless in my hand, hardly to listen the telephone advice from a friend of ours, by the name of Robert MERYC; advice which just advised me for example again: "... / ... And if she dies! Alberto Rodriguez also could "die"! ". Advice which just advised me for example again: "At this moment all your life! Or to better express it myself: all the rest of your life, you could for example have to ... / ...!". Advice which just advised me by example again: "You could for example, "have to suffer with your own consciousness"! In this case!". Advice which just advised me by example again: ""In this case, it would be": "The Other Form of Torture Of Your Own Conscience"!". A bitter refusal; categorical and unrelenting to listening them on my behalf; then I accelerated and consequently; *and consequently! That's all: And consequently!*, (, and this without even so far, I realizing it myself) my present total loss.

""That's all right: Indeed!, agreed!" ""IRENE will never, ever, never, ever; and never, ever, never, ever, stop at all, at all, to say, say, say, uncontrolled words, making them completely lose the North.

""That's all right: Agreed!, Indeed!!" ""IRENE would never, ever, never, ever; and never, ever, never, ever, stop so to speak, ever now: singing; singing; singing; singing sadly even in the air; singing nostalgically even in the air:

"Aurora;
Cãlium;
Purpurã.

Tempère;
Trõndõre;
Amarre;
Sõndõre.

Expulsa;
Rãpidãmantõ;
Quetõdã.

Diminuãwõn;
Quãntitãõn;
Fanrãwõn;
Sononrãwõn!

Alberto;
Adelino JACINTA.
Rodriguez;
Elisio RODRIGUEZ GOMEZ;
Adriano CARDOZO;
Eliodoro RODRIGUEZ;
Irene;
LUCINDAÇIO;
Edouardo FERNANDO!

RODRIGUEZ leaving "the BEUSCHERILVA".
"Avenida Morvan Branco".
"Avenida Otaviano Alves of Lima",
"Rua Olavo".
Canal "Rio Tieté".
Here = End of Life of Alberto

Secondly, the Future Businesswoman
Elisio RODRIGUEZ GOMEZ;
Elisio RODRIGUEZ GOMEZ, " the Future Businesswoman
ChanceKing (Queen) Emp (Empress)";
Elisio RODRIGUEZ GOMEZ, "a future wheeler guru";
Elisio RODRIGUEZ GOMEZ, "a future business guru".
Secondly, therefore, the future businesswoman
Elisio RODRIGUEZ GOMEZ; happened to be for
"the Blacks": "the very symbol of success";
"That symbol of success" that always sat still and
always, to work hard; in order to maintain their
Social Status; or: in order to gallop even Higher;
a symbol of success; which was "playing" in "the big leagues";
"Courtyard" which proved that again and again and continues
to prove to be always a Highly competitive Environment!

To go to the City Hall, to go and ask the
two Official Papers of Civil state!
And she ends its run on ["The Long Water The Serpentine"].
Here = End of Life of Elisio RODRIGUEZ GOMEZ

Elisio RODRIGUEZ GOMEZ narrowly missed to
become the future Director of "BEUSCHERILVA".
-What miss for me Irene LUCINDAÇIO and for all my family!
Was it not already there: "THE OTHER FORM OF
TORTURE OF HER OWN CONSCIENCE".

Aurora;
Cãlium;
Purpurã.

Tempère;
Trõndõre;
Amarre;
Sõndõre.

Expulsa;
Rãpidãmantõ;
Quetõdã.

Diminuãwõn;
Quãntitãõn;
Fanrãwõn;
Sononrãwõn!".

And one on of the best. And just happens to Aminata Ayichatoune of "Mali" is exactly; exactly! That's all exactly!, the same.

The heart, the heart, the heart of IRENE would prove to be completely lost.

The soul, the soul, the soul of IRENE would prove to be completely clueless.

And to be able to spice up this fury, the head of IRENE talked nonsense, talked nonsense, talked nonsense, of craziness;

The lower limbs of IRENE shaking, shaking, shaking the foolishness;

The Senior members of IRENE flickered, flickered, and flickered, the madness;

But quite frankly, the heart of IRENE would stop hardly at all, at all, throb, throb, and throb, frequently and most importantly, frantically, for nothing;

IRENE would not stop so to speak, ever, never now: to prove; to reveal; to reveal; to reveal herself indecently in the air;

to move; to move; to move; to move her body rhythmically, incorrectly, in the air;

to gesticulate; to gesticulate; to gesticulate; to gesticulate desperately in the air; almost everywhere, where she found herself.

Decidedly short, she spoke bitterly;

she spoke disrespectfully;

she spoke invalidly.

Brief ultimately, she spoke copiously! That's all: Copiously!, contemptuously;

she spoke undoubtedly! That's all: Undoubtedly!, wistfully;

she spoke explicitly! That's all: Explicitly!, poorly.

In short now, she Humed clearly! That's all: clearly explicitly!, irretrievably;

she Humed very clear; very clearly! That's all: Very clearly explicitly!, rudely;

she Humed copiously! That's all: Copiously!, awkwardly.

In short now, she sang undoubtedly! That's all: Undoubtedly!, irrevocably;

she sang copiously! That's all: Copiously!, disproportionately;

she sang copiously! That's all: Copiously!, darkly.

Decidedly short, she explicitly! That's all: Explicitly!, turned out obtrusively and wantonly;

she explicitly! That's all: Explicitly!, turned out recklessly and contemptuously;

she explicitly! That's all: Explicitly!, proved mechanically and impulsively.

Brief ultimately she explicitly! That's all: Explicitly!, moved uncomfortably;

she explicitly! That's all: Explicitly!, moved stolidly;

she copiously! That's all: Copiously!, moved unskilfully.

In short now, she copiously! That's all: Copiously!, gesticulated irreparably;

she copiously! That's all: Copiously!, gesticulated pathologically;

she copiously! That's all: Copiously!, gesticulated sickly.

She explicitly! That's all: Explicitly!, shuffled, she dragged one's feet, she been unable to shake off ridiculously home or elsewhere, whatever.

She explicitly! That's all: Explicitly!, walked decidedly it easy, take it easy, take it easy; she clearly! That's all: clearly explicitly!, walked soft, soft, soft; she very clear; very clearly! That's all:

Very clearly explicitly!, slowly walked decidedly; she explicitly! That's all: Explicitly!, even walked horribly now.

The heart of IRENE caught the arrhythmia.

Her heart was beating, beating, beating fast and improperly ("improperly" [so unsuitable]).

She undoubtedly! That's all: Undoubtedly!, waved, saluted, bowed politely and ridiculously vacuum; but according to her, they were people she had known in London; which had come to visit her; but that people unfortunately alas!, other people familiar with the knowing (the knowing her, IRENE) had consequently; *and consequently! That's all: And consequently*: not only never, ever seen before; but also that, even at times then the Irene greet; they do not see (and for them: IRENE would there often enough, but welcome the void, and that, with all the most distinguished bows, like those which are exhibited vis-à-vis the kings or the queens, for example).

And one on of the best. And just happens to Aminata Ayichatoune of "Mali" is exactly; exactly! That's all exactly!, the same.

While categorically refuse to eat food whose hers family members had giving to her; however IRENE would search garbage cans, to try to find food precisely, that she would pick up, to eat. She systematically refused decidedly, any assistance which one would give her, by her family. IRENE even refuses virtually any assistance from any other person whatever it may be;

so she was not herself;

so that she would become "remained";

so that she would become "mentally retarded";

so that she would become "siphoned off".

But as to herself Irene LUCINDAÇIO, she said very explicitly, explicitly! That's all: Explicitly!, to be normal. In other words, she seems to have her mind very, very; very, very well! That's all: Very, very well!, in good condition; and therefore, she systematically; *systematically! That's all: Systematically!*, refuse any help that they were trying to bring to her.

Irene LUCINDAÇIO tears herself pretty often and regularly, almost all her clothes; which ones she was wearing; and in doing so, she would walk in this case, almost as often and regularly naked and without shoes; but paradoxically; *"and paradoxically"! That's all: "And paradoxically"!*, the chill of the cold season, it apparently did nothing at her.

Irene LUCINDAÇIO would even have "the maggots" in all hers toes, so she lays in the wrecked vehicles, or on the land outright. Many times, her family would (2) {Despite her.} give to her, the treatment. But too many times, all of them would resume with a vengeance; so that her conscience was tortured.

Right in the "Camara of Lobos" [in the Isle of Madeira], for example, where we spoke virtually all yet in Portuguese, IRENE not be expressed as to her now than English in almost every street corner; where she stopped on purpose in order to take some pretty inconsistent, in the ears of people who listened; but consistent with her own ears.

Miss Irene LUCINDAÇIO, evokes; and that with a melodramatic, almost "all the hominids"; which ones, she had known; and among others especially Almeida LOURENÇO; Antonio Ferreira; Lopez Ramiro and Alberto Rodriguez; and "precisely which ones hominids had" greatly changed the course of her life. Of course! That's all: Of course!

Irene LUCINDAÇIO becomes simply "goofy". And without the neuropsychological cares, for her benefit, the delirium tremens of IRENE had simply multiplied again and again. And again and again. And yes ih! That's: Oll Korrect! Originally: An Astonishing natural acquired both attractive; than destructive: the beauty.

Before "becoming goofy," IRENE "became": "thin – skinned".

Having "been shines" IRENE "was saddlecloth".

Between "the states of obstinacy" IRENE "became wacko".

Otherwise wrote:

Before "becoming insane" IRENE "became": "disturbed".

After "the posting extravagance", IRENE "still showed amok".

Between "the states of rage", IRENE "showed even more of insanities".

Irene LUCINDAÇIO would continue with its frightening "chirps". And in this way, she would leave such to hear all those and all these who would indeed; that's all indeed!, agreed!, "comply" with her:"

""Between the camp of" "gentlewoman" and the camp of "gentleman" Church treasurer; we could not even suspect so slightly:"

"The suspicion and the hostility; "the enchantment" or "the sorcery" prevailing in both camps; which engendered a blind trust on the part "of the bimanous" of the "Surzur – Alvarez" Church."

"It was apparently not "falling out of love" beating the pavement and which promoted the show "hymeneal"; but rather: love. And it is therefore unnecessarily! That's all: Unnecessarily!, unnecessary, to express that "the Church treasurer's archetype" of the "Surzur – Alvarez" was damn wrong, and select:"

""The daughter of Jupiter and Aphrodite", as his wife; for what would follow would indeed, agreed; that's all agreed!, indeed!, be regarded as being such "a fiction" or else "a dream"; when in fact it was reality; or rather, the real magic."

"And yes ih! That's all correct! The magic making even broke into the mix! But what a story! This is the story of "a peripatetic", see!"

"It is not going to let me hear for example: That and yet, this is not "the finance" which "finance"."

""A girl card" that does not shy; it is really "a woman card" that will not shy!"

""A girl mistressesn" that does not shy; it is really "a woman mishandlesv" who will not shy!"

""A girl bitumen" that does not shy; it is really "a woman bitumen" who will not shy!"

""A girl wedding" that does not shy; it is really "a woman wedding" that will not shy!"

""A Girl on the Bridge" that does not shy; it is really "a woman on the Bridge" that will not shy!"

""A prostitute" who was not afraid of anything; it will truly "a public woman" who will not shy!"

""A prostitute" who was not afraid of anything; it is really "a woman of joy" who will not shy!"

""And cetera and cetera ....""

And one on of the best. And just happens to Aminata Ayichatoune of "Mali" is exactly; exactly! That's all exactly!, the same.

"And so, "the mercenary" is, however, end up closer than ever, never to its goal of "free riding" "of hard cashes" of the small Community of the Wake "the Surzur – Alvarez"."

"And so the life of "love market" is no longer a memory behind it; or rather, what's left as the memories."

"And everything went really, like for example: "this Mammy Water" in reality, is in the opposite "of the Church Treasurer – man" of the "Surzur-Alvarez", had its own vocabulary to her; like "the radish"; "the Round"; "the Welding"; "the wealth's"; "the readies"; "the tiles"; "the bubbles"; "the greens"; "the biscuits"; "the whites"; "the bobs"; and cetera and cetera ...."

"And this is even more true with the terms such as "the stew"; "the currency"; "the capital"; "the silver bread"; "the corner"; "the banknotes"; "the viaticum"; "the specie"; "the shekels"; "the mattress"; and cetera and cetera ...."

"And it is even higher, with the terms such as "the squandering"; "the Depredation"; "the Machination"; "the Ownership"; "the Breach of trust"; "the Prevarication"; "the giving as an excuse"; "the bribery"; and cetera and cetera …."

"All these terms were singing the "apology" of "the" Archduchess, "IRENE"; and of course, of course! That's all: Of course!, paradoxically, they sang "the Apocalypse" to "ALMEIDA", the Church treasurer – man of "the Surzur-Alvarez". A Reality heart touching, real, no!"

"And aye!, that's all OK!, "the bakers, such as between – others, me IRENE"! "The guys such as between – others: him ALMEIDA" should indeed, that's all indeed!, agreed!, as a result, expect everything!"

"The ideas of "diddle" really rang out in many brain freeze "this IRENE wolf, I am"."

"The question that "this Princess" herself arose as, while refusing very formally, to supply, were not that the premise of the response; but while touching wood:"

"How long "this knavery" "of funds" of the Church "Surzur – Alvarez" would last?"

""It would last only for a day!""

""For a week!""

""For a month!""

""For a quarter!""

""For a half!""

""For a year!""

"But, about how long exactly, exactly! That's all exactly!, masks "the streetwalkersn" fall?"

"And there, "the seemingly faithful wife without problem" would succeed in order to qualify this one precisely, the very, very; very, very well! That's all: Very, very well!, derogatory terms; such as:"

""The Bags pines"; "the Bollards bags"; "the slutsn"; "the bitch"; "the slut"; "the whore"; "the harlotsn"; "the hookersn"; "the pig"; "the mollsn"; and cetera and cetera. ..."

""And all these invectives then, ultimately succeed: a great silence.""

""The whoresn" always had and still always crossed on "the almighty dollar" and the scam looks."

""The swindling" and "the monkey business" in hiding! They are always well concealed, vis-à-vis the treasurer of the "Surzur – Alvarez" – "man of God"."

"Um mm! Against "the treasurer – man of God"."

"Here it still "poor" "blind", committed suicide by hanging!"

""The faithful who were hardly very reassuring, stood at a respectable distance.""

""The establishment terrified, wondering at this point more precisely:""

""What to do?""

""The funeral oration?""

""The Praise Hangman?""

""The Ballad of the Hanged Man?""

""The apology of treasurer integrates disillusioned?""

"Disillusioned by "pot" actually very focused on "the white metal" and "the bread – of – milk"?"

""A marmot" that felt much obliged to flee, flee and flee; far away; far; far, far away?"

"And in England, where she had found by chance, "the blind" is calling Alberto RODRIGUEZ?"

""For the baboons?""

""For the merits?""

""For the beauty?""

""For the felonies?""

""For even some grapes?""

""The marauding as it really needed?""

""The drabsn" finally, achieve exactly; exactly! That's all exactly!, "pass"?"

""The hostessesn»finally achieves exactly; affirmative! That's all affirmative!, "the accounts"?"

""The Flower sidewalk" finally, achieves exactly; obviously! That's all: Obviously!, "the stock"?"

""The whoresn" finally, achieves exactly; verily! That's all verily!, "the taffeta"?"

""The trollopsn" finally, achieves exactly; very well! That's all: Very well!, "the back wheel"?"

""The bawdsn" finally, achieves exactly; very, very well! That's all: Very, very well!, "the front wheel"?"

""The brutalizesv" finally, achieves exactly; that's all indeed!, agreed!, of the "the funds"?"

"In short, it is a story of "a bimanous" damned by the Church; and sentenced to the sufferings of hell!"

"In short, this is a story "of a bitch" who would not forgive "a guy" who did nothing but ask for the State – Civil Papers to "his Judith"!"

""In short, it is a history of the rancour or the bitterness for all the people mentioned here!""

""In short, it is a story of pain that lead to the worst, worst disasters!""

"In short, it is a story of Justice with a capital "J"; in other words: "The Justice Providential"!"".

""Take as an example!""

""Let's talk about the sudden unhealthy in the toilet where Irene Lucindaçio remained at last!""

""Which Irene, formerly cleaning woman well listed elsewhere, working for the accounts of the Temporary Agencies in London;""

""Which precisely cleaning woman, was polishing among others, the toilets, impeccably;""

""It was (and it was not surprising) past mistress in the matter of unhealthiness in question!""

""When she passed before other users of the same lavatories;""

""then!""

""Then! When someone else is saying for example:""

""I wanted to go to the toilet, quickly or not;""

""or to better express it:""

""I wanted to go to the needs of the front or rear;""

""(Whether it is front pee =;""

""What the fuck is or behind the poop);""

""It is grated, to be comfortable there;""

""There was placed before cause, Irene; and put them in full, next to where we had put!""

""And so you had for example (and only if it could be done without risk of destruction of health) at all;""

""Then really more at all, at all, so want to go to the waters!""

""And that ah!, that was really something eh! " """

And one on of the best. And just happens to Aminata Ayichatoune of "Mali" is exactly; exactly! That's all exactly!, the same.

I RENE would not stop so to speak, ever, never now: singing; singing; singing; singing sadly even in the air; singing nostalgically even in the air:

"Aurora;
Cãlium;
Purpurã.

Tempère;
Trõndõre;
Amarre;
Sõndõre.

Expulsa;
Rãpidãmantõ;
Quetõdã.

Diminuãwõn;
Quãntitãõn;
Fanrãwõn;
Sononrãwõn!

Alberto;
Adelino JACINTA.
Rodriguez;
Elisio RODRIGUEZ GOMEZ;
Adriano CARDOZO;
Eliodoro RODRIGUEZ;

Irene;
LUCINDAÇIO;
Edouardo FERNANDO!

RODRIGUEZ leaving "the BEUSCHERILVA".
"Avenida Morvan Branco".
"Avenida Otaviano Alves of Lima",
"Rua Olavo".
Canal "Rio Tieté".
Here = End of Life of Alberto

Secondly, the Future Businesswoman
Elisio RODRIGUEZ GOMEZ;
Elisio RODRIGUEZ GOMEZ, " the Future Businesswoman
ChanceKing (Queen) Emp (Empress)";
Elisio RODRIGUEZ GOMEZ, "a Future Wheeler Guru";
Elisio RODRIGUEZ GOMEZ, "a Future Business Guru".
Secondly, therefore, the Future Businesswoman
Elisio RODRIGUEZ GOMEZ; happened to be for
"the Blacks": "the very symbol of success";
"That symbol of success" that always sat still and
always, to work hard; in order to maintain their
Social Status; or: in order to gallop even Higher;
a symbol of success; which was "playing" in "the Big Leagues";
"Courtyard" which proved that again and again and continues
to prove to be always a Highly Competitive Environment!

To go to the City Hall, to go and ask the
two Official Papers of Civil State!

And she ends its run on ["The Long Water The Serpentine"].
Here = End of Life of Elisio RODRIGUEZ GOMEZ

Elisio RODRIGUEZ GOMEZ narrowly missed to
become the Future Director of "BEUSCHERILVA".
-What miss for me Irene LUCINDAÇIO and for all my family!
Was it not already there: "THE OTHER FORM OF
TORTURE OF HER OWN CONSCIENCE".

Aurora;
Cãlium;
Purpurã.

Tempère;
Trõndõre;
Amarre;
Sõndõre.

Expulsa;
Rãpidãmantõ;
Quetõdã.

Diminuãwõn;
Quãntitãõn;
Fanrãwõn;
Sononrãwõn!".

And one on of the best. And just happens to Aminata
Ayichatoune of "Mali" is exactly; exactly! That's all exactly!, the
same.

Irene Lucindaçio spoke, spoke, spoke, spoke and spoke again and again!

She trembled, trembled, trembled, trembled, and trembled again and again!

Her heart; her heart; her heart; her heart and heart beats still faster!

Only then, the clock was still going to turn for a while, before she could breathe her last.

Damsel demoiselle Irene LUCINDAÇIO would hold so two years to the day; and the beginning of the third year; and there, her account would be good: her body would be found lifeless in a wreck abandoned of vehicles.

And one on of the best. And just happens to Aminata Ayichatoune of "Mali" is exactly; exactly! That's all exactly!, the same.

For the record: we recall that Delilah – there, so named Irene LUCINDAÇIO, with "…/… Then her smile, talk – in fact. It is a constantly; *constantly! That's all: Constantly!,* smiling of Rebecca; to the point that one could imagine that she never, ever, never, ever; and never, ever, never, ever, being angry. When she laughs with the others, we need to go immediately to appropriate to her smile, to be – even, and therefore not for others. And especially when she smiles with you, we want to say that we fell in, madly in love. When she runs a bit and you observe the elongation of hers legs, you just feel happy. When she jokes with you, then – then, you feel like you be transported to the paradise. And the tone of her voice in all – there! So – there: it is another thing; it's another thing for it is a real melody like expressed by "the grannies – waters"; or even expressed by the heavenly angels.

In short, when Irene LUCINDAÇIO smiles; everyone smiles. And even when she farts; everybody farts.

-But Is that exactly, exactly! That's all exactly!, "the granny – water"?

But it is Irene LUCINDAÇIO!

In short, Irene LUCINDAÇIO: it is "an Angel – Heavenly – female" full crooked or bad habits.".

And it is "this bald – mouse – there precisely"; *precisely! That's all: Precisely!,* who died (; chastised so to speak: by "the invisible as powerful forces of Nature". [And how!]. [And why, 'there ah!]).

And it is very clear; very clearly! That's all: Very clearly explicitly!, "this real Siren – there precisely" who is dead!

And "that's true – true female angel from the Heaven", which is dead!

-Such a waste!

Indeed! That's all indeed!, agreed!: –What a squander!

"**I**rene Lucindaçio had completely lost the North; had completely lost the North! That's all: Had completely lost the North. Imitating supposedly, according to her, of course; of course! That's all: Of course!, Ma'am Lorena FLORINDA. Which one was doing so, the same."

"Irene Lucindaçio would stop so to speak, ever now: to reveal; to reveal; to reveal; to reveal herself indecently; indecently! That's all: Indecently!, in the air; imitating supposedly, according to her, of course; affirmative! That's all affirmative!, Bultez SULIVAN. Which one was doing so, the same."

"to move; to move; to move; of improperly; improperly! That's all: Improperly!, moving her body rhythmically; rhythmically! That's all: Rhythmically!, in the air; imitating supposedly, according to her, of course; obviously! That's all: Obviously!, Alfonso FUKIAKANDA. Which one was doing so, the same."

"to gesticulate; to gesticulate; to gesticulate; to desperately; desperately! That's all: Desperately!, gesticulating; gesticulating! That's all: Gesticulating!, in the air; virtually anywhere where he found himself. Imitating supposedly, according to her, of course; exactly! That's all exactly!, Adelaide Matumona. Which one was doing so, the same."

"In short really, Irene Lucindaçio used the art of the writing; used the art of the writing! That's all: Used the art of the writing. Imitating supposedly, according to her, of course; verily! That's all verily!, the writer Isaac MAMPUYA Samba. Which one was doing so, the same."

"In short really, Irene Lucindaçio bitterly spoke; bitterly spoke! That's all: Bitterly spoke!; imitating supposedly, according to her, of course; absolutely! That's all absolutely!, Imbourt GUERIN. Which one was doing so, the same."

"Irene Lucindaçio spoke irreverently; spoke irreverently! That's all: Spoke irreverently!; imitating supposedly, according to her, of course; very well! That's all: Very well!, Pastor Fernando Bezina. Which one was doing so, the same."

"Irene Lucindaçio spoke invalidly; spoke invalidly! That's all: Spoke invalidly. Imitating supposedly, according to her, of course; that's all indeed!, agreed!, Arnold Gutenberg Which one was doing so, the same."

"In short ultimately Irene Lucindaçio spoke disdainfully; spoke disdainfully! That's all: Spoke disdainfully!; imitating supposedly, according to her, of course; that's all agreed!, indeed!, Eugenio VENSIO. Which one was doing so, the same."

"Irene Lucindaçio spoke wistfully; spoke wistfully! That's all: Spoke wistfully!; imitating supposedly, according to her, of course; surely! That's all surely!, Agostinho Miguel. Which one had doing so, the same."

"Irene Lucindaçio was speaking poorly; was speaking poorly! That's all: Was speaking poorly. Imitating supposedly, according to her, of course; that's: Oll Korrect!, Ma'am Mikaella RENNECHEO. Which one was doing so, the same."

In short now, Irene Lucindaçio sang irreparably; sang irreparably! That's all: Sang irreparably!; imitating supposedly, according to her, of course; that's all correct!, Mr. Althino FERNANDE. Which one was doing so, the same."

Irene Lucindaçio sang rudely; sang rudely! That's all: Sang rudely!; imitating supposedly, according to her, of course; of course! That's all: Of course!, Ma'am Ana Valente. Which one was doing so, the same."

"Irene Lucindaçio Huming awkwardly; Huming awkwardly! That's all: Huming awkwardly. Imitating supposedly, according to her, of course; that's all OK!, Inacio DONZILA. Which one was doing so, the same."

"In short now, Irene Lucindaçio sang irrevocably; sang irrevocably! That's all: Sang irrevocably!; imitating supposedly, according to her, of course; absolutely! That's all absolutely!, Justino Djebali. Which one was doing so, the same."

"Irene Lucindaçio sang disproportionately; sang disproportionately! That's all: Sang disproportionately!; imitating supposedly, according to her, of course; certainly! That's all: Certainly!, Haman GENSEN. Which one was doing so, the same."

"Irene Lucindaçio sang darkly; sang darkly! That's all: Sang darkly. Imitating supposedly, according to her, of course; that's all right yes!, Antonio Ferreira. Which one was doing so, the same."

"In short really, Irene Lucindaçio proved worryingly; proved worryingly! That's all: Proved worryingly!, and immodestly; immodestly! That's all: Immodestly!; imitating supposedly, according to her, of course; that's right yes!, Sebastião VARGAS. Which one was doing so, the same."

"Irene Lucindaçio proved recklessly; proved recklessly! That's all: Proved recklessly!, and shamelessly; shamelessly! That's all: Shamelessly!; imitating supposedly, according to her, of course; that's right!, Luis Soarès Gracia. Which one was doing so, the same."

"Irene Lucindaçio proved mechanically; proved mechanically! That's all: Proved mechanically!, and impulsively; impulsively! That's all: Impulsively. Imitating supposedly, according to her, of course; Oll Korrect!, Stella-Maria HOBBONE. Which one was doing so, the same."

"In short now, Irene Lucindaçio gesticulated irreparably; gesticulated irreparably! That's all: Gesticulated irreparably!; imitating supposedly, according to her, of course; that's all indeed!, Joachim MENE. Imitating supposedly, according to her, of course; that's all affirmative!, JOÃO BARRAY-Santos. Which one was doing so, the same."

"Irene Lucindaçio gesticulated pathologically; gesticulated pathologically! That's all: Gesticulated pathologically!; imitating supposedly, according to her, of course; that's all absolutely!, Manuella LUCINDAÇIO. Which one was doing so, the same."

"Irene Lucindaçio gesticulated weakly; gesticulated weakly! That's all: gesticulated weakly. Imitating supposedly, according to her, of course; that's all exactly!, Silvao LUCINDAÇIO. Which one was doing so, the same."

"Irene Lucindaçio dragging, dragging and dragging; dragging and dragging! That's all: Dragging and dragging!; Irene Lucindaçio dragging, dragging and dragging, ridiculously; ridiculously! That's all: Ridiculously!, home or elsewhere, whatever. Imitating supposedly, according to her, of course; that's all agreed!, Amy Sophia LEBRETONA. Which one was doing so, the same."

"Irene Lucindaçio walked decidedly it easy, take it easy, take it easy; walked decidedly it easy, take it easy, take it easy! That's all: Walked decidedly it easy, take it easy, take it easy!; imitating supposedly, according to her, of course; that's all righto!, Elisio Gomez Rodriguez. Which one was doing so, the same."

"Irene Lucindaçio walked sweet, sweet, sweet; walked sweet, sweet, sweet! That's all: Walked sweet, sweet, sweet!; imitating supposedly, according to her, of course; that's all uh – huh!, Adelino JACINTA. Which one was doing so, the same."

"Irene Lucindaçio decidedly walked slowly; decidedly walked slowly! That's all: Decidedly walked slowly!; imitating supposedly, according to her, of course; that's all aye!, Eliodoro RODRIGUEZ. Which one was doing so, the same."

"Irene Lucindaçio walked same excruciatingly; walked same excruciatingly! That's all: Walked same excruciatingly!, now. Imitating supposedly, according to her, of course; that's all aye – aye!, Lopez Ramiro."

Her heart was beating, beating, beating fast; was beating, beating, beating fast! That's all: Was beating, beating, beating fast!, and improperly ("improperly"; "improperly"! That's all: "Improperly"!, [so that did not suit]; imitating supposedly, according to her, of course; that's all OK!, Alberto Rodriguez). Which one was doing so, the same."

"Irene Lucindaçio bowed, saluted, bowed politely; bowed, saluted, bowed politely! That's all: Bowed, saluted, bowed politely!, and ridiculously vacuum; ridiculously vacuum! That's all: Ridiculously vacuum!; there were people she had known before, who had come to visit her; imitating supposedly, according to her, of course; that's: Oll: Uh – huh!, Ma'am RAPHAËL RAFALA. Which one was doing so, the same."

"but that people unfortunately, alas!, the other people who know the knowing (; knowing her Irene Lucindaçio) had consequently not only never seen before; had consequently not only never seen before! That's all: Had consequently not only never seen before!; but also that, even at times then 'that Abdera greet them; imitating supposedly, according to her, of course; that's all yeah!, The Reverend Pastor Augy Wucher. Which one was doing so, the same."

"Irene Lucindaçio would there often enough, only welcome a vacuum; would there often enough, only welcome a vacuum! That's all: Would there often enough, only welcome a vacuum!; and this, with all the most distinguished possible bows; imitating supposedly, according to her, of course; that's all Okay!, Ernesto DOMINGUEZ ALMEIDA. Which one was doing so, the same."

"like the bows of which are exhibited vis-à-vis the Kings or Queens; like the bows of which are exhibited vis-à-vis the Kings or Queens! That's all: like the bows of which are exhibited vis-à-vis the Kings or Queens!, for example). Imitating supposedly, according to her, of course; of course! That's all: Of course!, Marta VITALINO. Imitating supposedly, according to her, of course; obviously! That's all: Obviously!, Barrene LUCINDAÇIO. Which one was doing so, the same."

"Once: Irene Lucindaçio had said very explicitly, be normal; had said very explicitly, be normal! That's all: Had said very explicitly, be normal. In other words: Irene Lucindaçio would say owning her mind very, very good condition; and therefore Irene Lucindaçio systematically; systematically! That's all: Systematically!, will refuse any help that they were trying to bring her. Imitating supposedly, according to her, of course;

verily! That's all verily!, Aziz OLENGA. Which one was doing so, the same."

"Another blow: Irene Lucindaçio eventually recognize: "That, Irene Lucindaçio was not Irene Lucindaçio herself. ". Imitating supposedly, according to her, of course; very well! That's all: Very well!, Fren Teach Montgo. Which one was doing so, the same."

"Irene Lucindaçio eventually recognize: "That, Irene Lucindaçio would become "remained"; would become "remained"! That's all: Would become "remained".". Imitating supposedly, according to her, of course; surely! That's all surely!, Bernadette Of The Sister Rosalie. Which one was doing so, the same."

"Irene Lucindaçio eventually, recognize: "That, Irene Lucindaçio would become "mentally retarded"; would become "mentally retarded"! That's all: Would become "mentally retarded". Imitating supposedly, according to her, of course; that's all indeed!, agreed!, José Manuel GLORIA.". Imitating supposedly, according to her, of course; of course! That's all: Of course!, Aminata Ayichatoune. Which one was doing so, the same."

"Irene Lucindaçio eventually recognize: "That, Irene Lucindaçio would become "siphoned off"; would become "siphoned off".! That's all: would become "siphoned off". Imitating supposedly, according to her, of course; that's all agreed!, indeed!, Camilo CARVALHO.". which one was doing so, the same."

"Irene Lucindaçio would simply become "thin-skinned"; would become "siphoned off".! That's all: Would become "siphoned off". And without neuropsychological care, delirium tremens; without neuropsychological care, delirium tremens! That's all: Without neuropsychological care, delirium tremens!, of Irene Lucindaçio had simply multiplied over and over. And again and again. And yes ih! Of course! Absolutely! That's all absolutely!, Imitating supposedly, according to her, of course; certainly! That's all: Certainly!, Claudio CAETANO. Which one was doing so, the same."... / ...!"".

"Irene Lucindaçio, did not hesitate to evoke this case of a certain gentleman ————; certainly! That's all: Certainly!, which one who showed himself; who showed himself; of course! That's all: Of course!, who showed himself; apparently very, very kindly (; and with many smiles in her mouth), in the eyes of people; but in truth, slyly, he is very, very, very dangerous. This Mr. ———————, is not even hesitating (for example, really: not at all at all [pushed, by his sly instinctive jealousy]; pushed, by his uncontrolled and unforgiving instinctive jealousy, or rather: by his uncontrolled sickly jealousy and without the smallest pity); to steal by the trickeries (at first Irrationals, and after that: rational 's), the works of the Writer Isaac MAMPUYA Samba [; who had had the misfortune, to trust "blindedly" and completely, him]; this gentleman tried to impose his name inside them, without speaking about it, to the! author who had too much, too much suffered to realize his works, appreciated by the world; no matter how: he would not agree to share the paternity of these latter's [; and this clever one, he knew it; hum mm! Try to impose his name in them, while he is not even himself, a writer. That ah! He really placed his challenge very, very, very high; and the Heaven not forgiving, at all, at all, such tricks; then: he had simply failed miserably. And yes ih! That's: Oll Korrect! Heavenly Justice exists, eh! Otherwise, hard, hard, hard."

(And without any pity at all, at all, while he was apparently laughing very, very well; very, very well! That's all: Very, very well!, with him, Isaac MAMPUYA Samba. And that's all right yes!, the person who hurts you is which one who surely! That's all surely!, eats; which one who drinks; which one who laughs; and one passes and the best] with you. The singers among others, have several times, evoked it; and the writers, too. And now in my turn, I Irene Lucindaçio, I evoke, I evoke, I evoke, I evoke, I evoke, and once more again, I also evoke this, about a certain gentleman –––––; obviously! That's all: Obviously!, who, by the Multiple tricks: first, Irrationals and then rational 's, he wanted the name of Isaac MAMPUYA Samba not at all to be imagined on his own works, but rather that of this gentleman –––– in question effectively! That's all effectively!. –What a hell of a world! That ah!)."

"Irene Lucindaçio, imitating, according to herself, obviously, this gentleman –––––––, who clearly! That's all: clearly explicitly!, showed himself, who showed himself, who very clear; very clearly! That's all: Very clearly explicitly!, appeared to be very, very, very likeable (; and with among others many of smiles at the mouth), in the eyes of people; but in truth, slyly, he is very, very, very dangerous."... / ...!"".

"Irene Lucindaçio, did not hesitate to say, to say, to say:"

"Afterwards, there is these clever 's people, who among the firsts, after all, arise among others the questions of knowing: - Where is this writer Isaac MAMPUYA Samba, which one, ([Indeed, agreed; that's all agreed!, indeed! : Isaac To Waddle and To Drum on MAMPUYA ; and MAMPUYA Sings and Dances of the Samba. DEMONSTRATION :]), he finds - therefore, his sources of inspiration? The answer being all clear and straightforward. For example, he does not even have to bend his body, to pick up these sources of inspiration on the floor. These clever 's men, precisely, serve them directly to him, on a tray; on a golden plate; on a solid golden plate; by their numerous petty tricks. And thus themselves: they fall down inevitably; and consequently, him Isaac MAMPUYA Samba who: He rises inexorably."... / ...!"".

And one on of the best. And just happens to Aminata Ayichatoune of "Mali" is exactly; exactly! That's all exactly!, the same.

If Miss Irene LUCINDAÇIO was able to forgive Alberto RODRIGUEZ; when it was still time; we would not perhaps yet arrived where we had come.

One had come where?

One had come where in disasters, many disasters.

One had come where?

One had come where at tragedies; the many tragedies.

And all these disasters; and all these tragedies 3 { : *[Spread the word!]*. }; that is to say:

The death of Ma'am Adelino JANCITA, the mother of Alberto RODRIGUEZ;

> the death of the young businessman Alberto RODRIGUEZ precisely; that is to say, himself the only son; and this fact: the heir;

> the death of Elisio GOMEZ RODRIGUEZ, "the Price of Diane" of Irene had been together, with A. RODRIGUEZ;

> and finally, the death of herself Irene LUCINDAÇIO 4 { : *It was so, had finished which one we had once dubbed "The daughter of Jupiter and Aphrodite. "*. };

without forgetting at the time: One of the four occupants of the Citroen which one was downright planned out through the windshield; and was therefore killed almost instantly. And: The three others occupants which ones were trapped inside their car; which began immediately to burn first little bit by little bit. They were well aware; and they cried even: "Help! Help! Help!". But alas!, unfortunately; *unfortunately, alas! That's all: Unfortunately, alas!*, by the time the firefighters who had been phoned and yet quickly!; and which came so quickly too; the only time they arrive on the scene of the accident, this Citroen Two Horses ' s car was downright exploded as a result of the fire which had for a few minutes, started to burn out little by little. The three people, who were trapped, were burned alive.

If so: Miss Irene LUCINDAÇIO was able to forgive Alberto RODRIGUEZ; when it was still time; we would not perhaps yet arrived where we had come.

All that, and all that, and all that, and all that, and all that, and all that,

were all, the direct consequences; the direct impacts, of "the contest untimely" of two circumstances:

On one hand, the breach of trust had demonstrated Irene LUCINDAÇIO herself vis-à-vis her "former husband" Almeida LOURENÇO. The latter had to endure a terrible humiliation 5.

{ : If it also; that is to say: Almeida LOURENÇO had to endure a terrible shame; a terrible indignity due to embezzlement of funds of the faithful, the "SURZUR – ALVAREZ", a small fledgling Reformed Church;

"Revival Church";

"an Awakened Church";

"a Revealed Church";

that is to say: "a Church Communicated by the Divine Revelation"; if we are to believe; or to better express it: if you referred according to "the words" of the followers of this fact;

So, if Almeida LOURENÇO had to endure a terrible shame due to the embezzlement of public funds of the practitioners, of a small Church which "grew" in the small Island of Madeira, in the years 1960; it was also, without really knowing it himself, "a Roundabout Way"; "A rather Irrational Way"; "a Supernatural method" to punish him, almost inadvertently, due to the fact that he used "unorthodox trick" in order to marry this one just likes her considerably; that is to say, that we had finally, nicknamed "The daughter of Jupiter and Aphrodite". By diverting money from the Church, for "his parishioner Irene LUCINDAÇIO"; though he would divorce with her, "the poor" Almeida LOURENÇO no one had hardly, recovered from this sad affair. "The unfortunate" had just committed suicide on a certain night, by hanging. }. And unfortunately alas!, unfortunately, alas! That's all: Unfortunately, alas!, before this terrible tarnish caused by the misappropriation of Church's funds, by "his parishioner Irene LUCINDAÇIO"; though he would divorce with her, "the poor" Almeida LOURENÇO no one had hardly recovered from this sad affair. "The unfortunate" had just committed the suicide some night by hanging.

And unfortunately, alas! ; unfortunately, alas! It is simply: Alas, unfortunately!; *unfortunately, alas! That's all: Unfortunately, alas!*, in front of this terrible tarnish engendered As who would say:

Like who would say:

"**A**s who would say:" This is what we would call in the Cosmic or Astral or Extra – Galactic Jargon: THE COSMIC DISILLUSION; or rather: THE COSMIC ILLUSION "; for not to say: "This is what we would call in the Mystic Language or in the Language of the Cryptogram or of Black-out or of the Martingale: THE MYSTICAL ARCANS; or rather: THE MYSTERIES OF THE UNIVERSE".

—Isaac MAMPUYA Samba

In fact, that's what IsMaSa would call "The Pole"; hence: the discovery of the "Pole". Otherwise expressed: "the Pot"; "The Rose Pot"; hence so: " the discovery of the "Roses pot" of the "Pink Pole". ».

Let us listen, therefore, to Irene LUCINDAÇIO, on this subject: "In any case, I Irene LUCINDAÇIO, I bear the bad lucky, to the people. That is to say, I had already, already, already, already and already, introduced the redoubtable idea of: "The Suicidero – Form"; "the Suicidero 's form"; through "the sad – form"; by "the nostalgia – form"; and "the melancholy – form", in a peaceful family of Thirteen people ([the LOURENÇO's family]: the offspring and their parents); which Thirteen people precisely; *precisely! That's all: Precisely!,* had completely "suicidality, so to speak" decimated. "And what was the use of this macabre idea because of who? It was because of me Irene LUCINDAÇIO. But really: –What rubbish I am? So, I must be ashamed to be able to look at myself, in a mirror!".

Unfortunately, unfortunately; *unfortunately, alas! That's all: Unfortunately, alas!,* in front of this terrible tarnish engendered

As the great Madam Lorena Florinda, just she would have said about this Irene LUCINDAÇIO and this Bernadette of The Sister Rosalie; or rather: of this Aminata AYICHATOUNE: "In short, the maintenance of the Parakeets (which they work themselves and receive wages [prodigious or not]: whatever) costs very, very dear to their Parrots. For this purpose, they must put: a lot of cashes and still a lot of cashes; and especially for the Sirens – Parakeets; then! So, in fact, be wary! Be wary really!".

And secondly, it was that one Alberto Rodriguez had finally, nicknamed: "Thousand Stars".

Now if he had known this sad affair was a result of the fact that he had "an old V – W Ladybird"; which he was ultimately impossible to pull off without adverse consequences; which would ensure surely! That's all surely!, that he no longer has a residence permit; or rather, the Papers to stay in England, in rules.

But if A. RODRIGUEZ possessed "an old V – W Beetle", it was because he had the "graciously" offered as a reward by a "Sir" Haman GENSEN, because of "his actually false testimony"; to save his honour; while flipping through it actually quite sad; by this heinous act; and this, in rather sad and rather pathetic situations, the life of a couple innocent; or to put it in another way: by doing so much harm: both directly and indirectly to Ma'am Valery GLED, wife REDLER; to her husband: "Sir" Lancry REDLER; and do not forget: to their two children which ones they had at the time, in charge; which had seen of that way – there, tearing their parents (6). { : *Cfr.: Isaac Mampuya Samba: "Irene LUCINDAÇIO, the daughter of Jupiter and Aphrodite".* }.

Like what!!!

In short, about Stephanie and Augustus (to see them - so, very, soon): it would begin with the story of a thunderbolt and an euphoric climax; and it would rapidly turn by a history of docked insaneness schizophrenia and the end apocalyptic.

-What Unprecedented journey to a question of love!

At the culmination of "the ride" from "Two Events" (again), it turns very, very palpably the approach: that a story of Justice with a capital "J"; in other words: "The Justice Providential" does not even palaver.

IsMaSa

————makes talking pen;

————makes commiserating writing.

Indeed, agreed : Isaac To Waddle and To Drum on MAMPUYA ; and MAMPUYA Sings and Dances of the Samba. DEMONSTRATION:

* * *

THE END

For almost "all this writing lying below high" "with the black anchor on a white background or a white paper"; namely: that there are among others; or to be able to say more correctly: they were then among – others: "the imaginary stories"; which are much more similar to "the real stories" rather than anything else; i.e.: they are then among – others; or in order to better express it: they were then among – others: "the true stories"; which are much more similar to "the imaginary stories" rather than anything else.

"AUGUSTUS AND STEPHANIE ... / .... ".

All the readers who wish to continue their reading in the "BaLiSambaSty" are invited to read the next volume due out small; and which will be titled:

"AUGUSTUS AND STEPHANIE: A CURIOUS GOOD AND MYSTERIOUS CROSSROADS".

"AUGUSTUS AND STEPHANIE:
A CURIOUS GOOD AND
MYSTERIOUS CROSSROADS".

**"NOTHING WOULD NOT ENTIRELY
BETWEEN TWO YOUNG LOVERS
BELGIAN: STEPHANIE AND "AUGUSTUS
OF REAR – OFFSPRING CONGOLESE"".**

PREAMBLE

Augustus Sebillon was in the 1980s, "a Security Agent" in the Offices – building at a site of Schaerbeek, in Belgium. He greatly enjoyed his work; and consequently, he did it very, very well. Very, very well! That's all: Very, very well! In their box, located in the entrance of the site, on the left, of "Security Agents" received a lot of people.

It is precisely; *precisely! That's all: Precisely!*, in that context, that "the guardian" AUGUSTUS receives a Saturday morning, in the full winter, a some computer scientist: Miss Stephanie BARREL. The latter would get "some understanding" about her score for hours, even more, that there was not during that time in their Establishment, the unit flextime. STEPHANIE would get "this arrangement" with "the Security Agent" that was on duty that day, in case: Augustus Sebillon.

The latter, carefully following the instructions of his work; he would not at all accept, to help Miss Stephanie BARREL. But that's only after insistence thereof; even after "blackmail" exercised against him, for one, Augustus, who from the start had already committed some fault; he would be in some so, in "this unfortunate obligation to" accept "the arrangement" by complacency.

But alas!, unfortunately; *unfortunately, alas! That's all: Unfortunately, alas!,* this irresponsible on his part, would cost!:

and his own place;

and quite logically, that of STEPHANIE.

She was a very good computer scientist, and so, she would not hurt to find another job "of computer science", in another Company in the same branch almost; than where she used to work.

But as for Augustus Sebillon, it would be "a real rubbish". He could not find the work at all, at all. He would suffer greatly, so much that he would even make the "handle" in the public transport, in order to survive. In order to get out once and for all, of this sad situation, where there was AUGUSTUS (2) { *: As the height of paradox.* }, the contest of Miss Stephanie BARREL, would be for him *necessarily! That's all: Necessarily!,* necessary, if not decisive precisely.

This new situation would ensure surely! That's all surely!, that Augustus and STEPHANIE eventually would form a couple, and live as a consequence, conjugal.

However, given all the miseries that had crossed Augustus Sebillon, he would "deliberately" ruthless revenge; but that does not even say her name, against "his Baroness STEPHANIE", which he considered (3) { *: Always almost slyly.* } be the responsible for the plight, which one he had passed through, with all the tarnishes that resulted; despite the fact that, she was STEPHANIE herself, which helped him to be able, to get by, ultimately.

Wanting ... / ...

"Want to walk his mind;

the escape into a world;

in a world of imagination;

imagination in retrospect;

retrospection that clings infallibly in the present;

a present that will grab turn tirelessly in the future;

in the future and around the world;

this is ultimately our best inclination.".

In short, Isaac MAMPUYA Samba is: "The Difference Blondinian or Hollywoodian or even downright planetary the most original in simplicity and humility of Scripture therefore which one can so exist. Otherwise expressed : That's the distinction, what!".

Signed: Isaac MAMPUYA Samba.

The Solitary Writer, with the Steel Pencil; or rather: at the Golden Pen.

NOVELS OF THE SAME AUTHOR

1 - " A True untimely Awareness".

2 - " Nervous Breakdown and Sorrow of Love".

3 - "Torment of "JULIO, Descent From Poitvese"".

4 - " An Ultimate Therapy To Save Their Children".

5 - "Impacts of the "Other Justice"".

6. – "Irene LUCINDAÇIO, the daughter of Jupiter and Aphrodite". (BEGINNING).

7. – "Irene LUCINDAÇIO, the daughter of Jupiter and Aphrodite". (CONTINUATION).

8. – "IRENE AND AN OTHER FORM OF TORTURE OF HER OWN CONSCIENCE". (BEGINNING).

9. – "IRENE AND AN OTHER FORM OF TORTURE OF HER OWN CONSCIENCE". (CONTINUATION).

ALSO FROM ISAAC MAMPUYA SAMBA:

1: Survival And Punishment Of The Slave Trade From Gabon until Congo in 1840 – 1880 (VOLUME ONE).

2: Survival and Repression Of The Slave Trade From Gabon until Congo in 1840 – 1880 (VOLUME TWO).

3: Survival and Penalty Of The Slave Trade From Gabon until Congo in 1840 – 1880 (VOLUME THREE).

4: Survival And Sentence Of The Slave Trade From Gabon until Congo in 1840 – 1880 (VOLUME FOUR).

5: The Relations Franco – Belgians 1884 – 1885: (Congo Affairs).

"Series or Sub-Series: "…/… Their Membership Negritude in Africa and in the World …/…"".

ABOUT THE BOOK

7. – "IRENE AND AN OTHER FORM OF TORTURE OF HER OWN CONSCIENCE". (CONTINUATION).

In this Volume of Isaac MAMPUYA Samba (IsMaSa) entitled: "IRENE AND AN OTHER FORM OF TORTURE OF HER OWN CONSCIENCE" (published by IsMaSa – Publishing, London – Paris – Los Angeles [With "(Published by "The Editions IsMaSa, London – Paris – Los Angeles" [With:

Publisher:AuthorIsaMAMSam-UK-USA

(["isaac.mampuya@laposte.net"]), several tragedies "would" succeed one by one; and end at Irene LUCINDAÇIO. Many "contests" in circumstances; starting with "herself IRENE" who, thinking only obtain by any means, materials and numerical foremost interests, it had resulted in the suicide of her former husband Almeida LOURENÇO:

"The whole thing was indeed; that's all indeed!, agreed!, started by those IRENE myself, I made to my first "anthropoid ALMEIDA". And all the calamities who follow, me until that time – here and that is to say: boosted by my meeting with Alberto Rodriguez, are only the workouts, or rather "the adversities" attracted by the old "fatalities" "latent's".""

And they would continue in addition, because of an ALBERTO that, to save his honour for a "blunder", and yet he had committed himself, he preferred to deliberately make very, very wrong to one innocent lady (Madam Valery GLED, wife REDLER] who had done nothing objectionable.

"And I ALBERTO, I did it, against "an Eva" like this? In order to save my honour?

Following a "blunder", and yet I had committed myself?

And as a reward, "Sir" Haman GENSEN gave to me "the famous V – W Beetle"?

Which, subsequently, had cause to me, too many disasters?")

In short, the "competition" of the circumstances "would" therefore be intertwined [; and these, pushed by an Invisible, Powerful Force] so unfortunately lead to "a Vicious and Dramatic Gear!"; which would generate Four Stiffs. But just when he was still ample time, while you could still obviously; obviously! That's all: Obviously!, stop them. How? By knowing step back and thinking very well. Very well! That's all: Very well! But that's only!!!

$\mathbf{I}$rene Lucindaçio and Alberto Rodriguez, as a result of the outrages, which ones, they themselves had committed, they would be Para - Normally speaking, Mysteriously; *"mysteriously"! That's all: "Mysteriously"!*, persecuted and tormented.

If Mademoiselle Irene LUCINDAÇIO had forgiven Alberto RODRIGUEZ; when there was still time; it might not have happened where we had arrived.

Where had we arrived?

At disasters, many disasters.

Where had we arrived?

To tragedies; many tragedies.

And all these catastrophes; and all these tragedies; that is to say:

The death of Ma'am Adelino JANCITA, the mother of Alberto RODRIGUEZ;

> the death of young businessman Alberto RODRIGUEZ precisely; *precisely! That's all: Precisely!*; that is to say, he himself the only son; and therefore: the heir;

> the death of Elisio GOMEZ RODRIGUEZ, "the price of Diane" that IRENE had had together with A. RODRIGUEZ;

> and finally, the death of herself Irene LUCINDAÇIO;

And about A. RODRIGUEZ: not forget to mention at the time: the four occupants of the Citroën that was squared out, through the windshield; and she was therefore killed almost instantly by accident.

If so: Mademoiselle Irene LUCINDAÇIO had forgiven Alberto RODRIGUEZ; when there was still time; it might not have happened where we had arrived.

All this, and all that, and all that, and all that, and all that, and all that, were all, the direct consequences; the direct repercussions of the "untimely competition" of two circumstances:

On the one hand, of the breach of trust that had been shown, Irene LUCINDAÇIO herself, vis-à-vis her "former husband": Almeida LOURENÇO. The latter must have suffered a terrible humiliation. And sadly, alas! In the face of this terrible tarnish caused by the embezzlement of church money, by his parishioner Irene LUCINDAÇIO; although he was divorced with this one, "the poor man" Almeida LOURENÇO had hardly recovered from this sad affair. "The unfortunate" had simply committed suicide a certain night, (a certain night, of a certain Friday the 13th), by hanging himself. In short, and as a result, this idea of suicide on the Fridays 13, was thus penetrated within a peaceful family of Thirteen people.

And on the other hand, from what Alberto RODRIGUEZ had finally nicknamed: "Thousand Stars."

IN BRIEF

---MORALITY OF THE STORY?

---Yes! Let's talk about it --- so indeed (; and of course, in the manner of Isaac MAMPUYA Samba).

IRENE (daughter of very, very poor parents), through her repeated burglaries of the Church's money "Surzur --- Alvarez", had indirectly caused the suicide of Almeida LOURENÇO (; whose the Ectoplasm on IRENE was decidedly everywhere at once and at the same time, nowhere).

RODRIGUEZ, son of very, very rich parents (; and through lack of vigilance, which he was pursuing while studying law in England, had inadvertently caused the theft of a package of great sentimental value; for which, he had consequently (in order to save his honour) unjustly accused an innocent lady: Mrs. Valery GLED, wife of REDLER); thus generating immeasurable consequences in her marital home.

---And the power of Karma in all these ---?

Irene had therefore made her decision of not to forgive Alberto Rodriguez (in his quest for civil status papers in England); her tongue was practically loose, and she had no pity. She was indifferent to Rodriguez's many cries and tears.

As a result of such an irrefutable decision by Irene, Rodriguez's body had become pale and devoid of all melanin. Thus, his face would never regain its usual melanin at all (; then really: his face would never regain its usual melanin at all); and what's more, he would never regain his appetite, which he had also lost. And in the end, he wouldn't get out of his live; and he would die.

And what about Irene? In short, the COSMIC VISION or THE CELESTIAL DECISION would also be indifferent to IRENE's many cries and tears.

The Fate had thus arranged for the paths of a certain Irene LUCINDAÇIO and a certain Almeida LOURENÇO to cross. But here's the thing: between the Two of them, there's going to be some dagger-drawn excitement.

————COINCIDENCE?

————Maybe so!

————Or even maybe not!

But nevertheless, after having read the THREE PREVIOUS IRENEs very, very carefully, one would clearly understand that one would not believe in Coincidence, as far as we are concerned here; because: the COSMIC VISION or THE CELESTIAL DECISION therefore really exists. The Proof.

THE BOUQUET OF NUMERICAL FLOWERS!

"**A**lthough by more experiences of the Scripture, the distinction "of the sonny of the Municipality of Ndjili; in the City of Kinshasa, in the Democratic Republic of Congo"; the elegance "of the son of the Metropolitan of Paris in France"; the perfection "of the boy from the Acropolis of Leeds and the Megalopolis of London, in Great Britain"; until: at "his landing – living", in Atlanta [Georgia – United – State]; (which son [; that is to say: Isaac MAMPUYA Samba] who offers his sensational literary wonders, or rather: his astonishing, to the World); this perfection precisely; precisely! That's all: Precisely!, is not, without making the happiness of the bulimics of the good readings! We would thus see in Internet, that: A Notoriety very, very Popular Planetary in Scripture:

> At characters, certainly: Literary, but not only. "Not only"; it is because also: To characters, Romantic's. But not only. "Not only"; it is because also: To characters, Monographic. But not only. "Not only"; it is because also: To characters, Retrospective. But not only. "Not only"; it is because also at last: To characters, Unexplored of the Writer Isaac

MAMPUYA samba is actually confirmed ... / ....
And that ah!, It's the Bouquet of Digital Flowers!
It really is: The Bouquet of Numerical Flowers,
that ah!"

Signed: Isaac MAMPUYA Samba.

HERE MARKS UP THEREFORE
THE END OF THIS SUB – SERIES CALLED:
IRENE (TREATED IN FOUR EPISODES).

The 4th Of Cover

The Writer Isaac MAMPUYA Samba

www.ingramcontent.com/pod-product-compliance
Lightning Source LLC
Chambersburg PA
CBHW031957120726
47898CB00002BA/550